SHUNNED *and* Embraced

THE CHIEFTAIN'S GIFTED WIFE

BY
BREE WOLF

Shunned & Embraced – The Chieftain's Gifted Wife
by Bree Wolf

This is a work of fiction. Names, characters, businesses, places, brands, media, events, and incidents are either the products of the author's imagination or used in a fictitious manner.

Any resemblance to actual persons, living or dead, or actual events is purely coincidental.

E-Book ISBN: 978-3-96482-124-9
Paperback ISBN: 978-3-96482-125-6
Hardcover ISBN: 978-3-96482-126-3

www.breewolf.com

SHUNNED *and* Embraced

THE CHIEFTAIN'S GIFTED WIFE

Chapter One

A HUNTER

The Highlands, Scotland 1755 (or a variation thereof)

The mist hung heavy over the ancient forest, tendrils of fog snaking around the broad trunks of gnarled oaks and towering pines. Damp earth and moss muffled Maeve's soft footsteps as she made her way silently through the trees, her hood drawn up over her fiery auburn hair and a heavy pack upon her back. Her green eyes darted cautiously, taking in every detail of her surroundings. She moved like a ghost, blending seamlessly into the forest that sheltered her, her wide cloak and simple gown mimicking the colors around her, greens and browns winding together into something that belonged.

Maeve paused, her breath catching at the snap of a twig underfoot, and her heart pounded in her chest as she listened intently for any sign of movement. Yet the only sounds to drift to her ears were the soft calls of birds and the whisper of the wind as it whistled through the leaves overhead, carried here from places far away.

After long moments, Maeve let out a shaky breath and then

continued on. She could never fully relax out here alone, not with the threat of discovery always looming. People were dangerous; Maeve had learned so early on. She tried her best to keep herself hidden, not to stray too close to any village if she could prevent it, and yet sometimes it could not be avoided. In these moments, fear held her body rigid as her mind struggled to keep at bay the awful memories that lingered at the edge of her thoughts.

Aye, once she had had a family and lived among people.

But no more.

Now, at no more than eighteen years of age, the forest was her home.

It was all she had now.

She had been Maeve Wallace once.

Now, she was simply Maeve.

With no family to call her own.

As Maeve ducked under a low-hanging branch, a raven cawed overhead, making her jump. She scowled up at it. "Are ye following me just to torment me, ye wee devil?"

The raven gave a raspy croak in reply, its eyes soulful, making Maeve wonder about the way it saw the world. Did it wonder about her the same way she wondered about it? Did it look at her thinking what sort of odd creature she was?

Shaking her head, Maeve turned away, reminding herself that she could not afford to lose focus out here. Not when her survival depended on staying alert. She had to keep moving, had to stay ahead of the dangers that pursued her. Dangers far worse than ravens or wolves...

With a weary sigh, Maeve pushed onward through the mist, determined to survive another day alone. Eventually, she paused beside a rocky stream, kneeling to splash some of the crisp, cold water on her face. Yet as she cupped her hands in the rushing water, her eyes caught on her reflection and a heavy sigh drifted from her lips.

It had been a long time since she had last seen her reflection, seen it clearly, her eyes bright green and her expression one of joy and cheerfulness. Aye, once she had been happy.

In some distant corners of her mind, memories lingered of smiles and laughter, of warm embraces and kind words, words of love even.

Only many years had passed since.

Now, Maeve hardly recognized the hollowness in her own gaze, the lingering shadows that seemed to trail over her features as though wishing to remind her of all that she had lost. Would she never forget? Maeve had wondered about this more than once, never quite certain what answer she hoped for. Indeed, some of her memories were beautiful, and yet now they were tinged with sadness and regret. Still, did she wish to abandon them, lose them, give them up for good? Were they not the only precious things she had left?

Years had passed since she had been forced from her home, accused of being witch for the strange power she possessed. She had been no more than a wee lassie, a child. Yet people had shown her no mercy, not even for one so young. The memory of the villagers' hateful cries still echoed in her mind, their faces twisted in fear and disgust as they had come for her. "Monster! Devil's spawn!"

Maeve squeezed her eyes shut against the painful memories. She had lost everything—her family, her home. Forced to flee into the wilderness or face the pyre.

Taking a shuddering breath, Maeve rose and continued foraging along the stream's edge. She plucked some wild onions and greens, expertly selecting only the edible plants. Though once a simple crofter's daughter, she had become adept at surviving on her own out here. After all, she had no other choice. Not truly at least. Or was survival a choice one made? Maeve was uncertain.

As she gathered food, her thoughts turned to her strange abilities, the curse that had condemned her. She could hear people's thoughts as though they were her own, dancing through her head in imitation of the voice that slipped from her throat. At first, Maeve had not even known these thoughts to be someone else's. They had confused her, to be sure. Yet it had taken some time for her to understand that somehow another's mind had entered her own, leaving behind a piece of itself. It had been nothing conscious, nothing she had intentionally done or sought to do. It had simply happened, and she had been unable to prevent it.

As far as Maeve had been able to unearth in the years since she had first taken notice, proximity made her curse more powerful. The closer someone stood to her, the louder his or her thoughts rang in her head. Yet it was not simply closeness of location. Indeed, her parents' and her younger siblings' thoughts had been most prominent upon her mind whether they had stood right beside her or far across the village with many people standing between them and her. Aye, closeness of the heart mattered as well.

At first, Maeve had been simply intrigued. Unsettled, to be sure. Yet her innocent mind had not on its own strayed to something evil. Only when she had begun to speak of it had her perception of her ability turned. Aye, Maeve remembered her mother's frightful expression upon first hearing her daughter speak of such a thing. She remembered her father insisting she keep it a secret and not mention it again. At not even ten years of age, Maeve had tried to heed her parents' warnings, and yet her young mind had been too intrigued.

And then she had taken one wrong step and...

Shaking off her dark reflections, Maeve moved deeper into the misty forest. She had to keep going, keep surviving. What else could she do? She was alone in this world now, with only the ancient trees as her companions.

Somewhere in the distance, a raven cawed once more as if reminding her that it, too, stood at her side, and a soft smile graced Maeve's lips as she made her way through the dense forest. The trees rose like silent sentinels all around her, their gnarled branches disappearing into the low-hanging mist. She took a deep breath, inhaling the rich, earthy scents—the mustiness of fallen leaves, the sharp tang of pine, the clean smell of the damp soil.

These woods felt more like home than any place she had known. Here, she did not have to hide who she was. The trees did not judge or condemn her for her strange ability. They simply accepted her, offering solace and shelter within their ancient embrace.

Maeve placed a hand against the rough bark of an oak. "If only ye could speak," she murmured. "Then I'd have someone to talk to." She smiled ruefully. Was she truly so desperate for companionship that she was talking to trees now?

Ever since she had been cast out, she had yearned for somewhere to belong, for someone who would understand her. Aye, Maeve knew that companionship with other people was something she would never have. She had lost the only family she had ever had, and she did not dare seek out others more often than need be for fear of their reaction. Still, occasionally, she dreamed of simply exchanging a few words here and there. Was that perhaps why she spoke to the animals and trees? To hear her own voice and remember that she was still here? That she had not perished somewhere deep in the woods?

If only she could speak to the animals or rather they could speak to her. Yet whether they possessed thoughts of their own, thoughts similar to those of people, Maeve could not hear them. Nay, their minds remained quiet and far away from her own, leaving her utterly alone in a world where she was not wanted.

Maeve froze as again the snapping of a twig cut through the silence. Her breath caught in her throat as she scanned the misty forest. Had she imagined it? Or was someone else out here?

She listened intently, her body tense. There—another crackle of leaves, too heavy to belong to a raven or a rabbit. Maeve's heart pounded, and her right hand went to her belt, silently unsheathing the dagger she kept there. It was her only protection against the wild, against anything or anyone who wished to do her harm. Yet, she knew quite well that it was not much.

On quiet feet, Maeve darted behind the thick trunk of an ancient oak. She slowed her breathing, willing her frantic heart to still, wondering if the sounds she heard belonged to a grazer or perhaps a predator.

Carefully, Maeve peaked around the trunk, her gaze drawn ahead to a soft rustling in the underbrush.

And then she saw it.

Colors that did not rightly belong in the forest. At least not in these shades.

Aye, in autumn, leaves showed shades of red while blue hues could be seen in rippling waters or brilliant skies. Yet in this moment, neither color was where it was supposed to be.

"Footsteps," Maeve murmured under her breath as she stared

through the thicket at the moving colors, now certain that it was no animal she was facing. Nay, it was a man judging by the heavy thud of his steps.

Maeve's heart flew into a panic as the footsteps grew louder, grew closer, accompanied every now and then by an almost guttural growl that made Maeve think of hungry wolves on the hunt.

Yet it was a man, and her mind raced through her options. Was she to flee deeper into the woods? Confronting him, of course, was out of the question. Nay, she could not let him see her. That would only lead to questions, suspicions... torches and pitchforks.

The footsteps halted, close now, and Maeve glimpsed a shadowy figure through the trees. Tall, broad-shouldered, with a shock of pitch-black hair.

The very moment Maeve spotted him, the man's thoughts emerged as a rumble in her mind, like distant thunder. Maeve clenched her fists and pinched her eyes shut, pushing back against his mind with every bit of strength she had. She could not afford to slip, to let her ability loose, for it confused her mind and twisted the world. Whenever another's thoughts rummaged through her head, Maeve no longer knew who she was. She felt robbed of every conscious thought, unable to clear her mind and use it as she otherwise would. In a word, she felt helpless.

The man turned, peering into the woods. Looking for her? Maeve shrank back against the oak, relieved to find that the shadows and fog shrouded her. Her hands remained clenched, and she gritted her teeth, fighting against the onslaught of the man's thoughts.

After a moment, the man continued on his way.

Maeve released a shaky breath. That had been close. Too close. She had to be more careful, keep her guard up. Clearly, the Highlands were not as empty as they seemed.

Only when the sound of footsteps had completely faded did she slip from her hiding place and pick her way silently through the trees, moving in the opposite direction from the mysterious man. Her pulse still thrummed, but she forced herself to focus, drawing deep breaths into her lungs. Surviving alone required vigilance and skill. She could not let fear override her instincts.

Kneeling, Maeve inspected some promising plants nestled between tree roots. Chanterelles. Perfect. She harvested the orange fungi with deft fingers, tucking them into a pouch on her belt. Food for tonight, and perhaps some to dry for harder times.

Satisfied with her find, Maeve stood and continued deeper into the misty forest. She kept her senses alert, listening for any signs of animals or, heaven forbid, people. Solitude was her ally, her protector. As long as she remained hidden, she was safe.

A clearing opened up ahead, dotted with scraggly bushes. Maeve recognized the oval leaves immediately—blueberries. A smile touched her lips, and she hurried forward, plucking the ripe berries and savoring their sweet-tart juice. They would make a fine dessert after the chanterelle stew.

For the first time since her close call with the man, Maeve's shoulders relaxed, for the familiar work of gathering food centered her. She had survived this long on her own. After all, she was a child of this forest—and the forest provided for its own.

By the time Maeve finished harvesting the blueberries, her fingers were stained purple. As she stood, a raven's hoarse cry echoed overhead, and she glanced up, watching the glossy bird alight on a nearby evergreen bough. "Hello, wee rascal," Maeve called on a laugh, savoring the sound. "'Tis good to see ye again."

The raven cocked its head, regarding her with one obsidian eye, as though it objected to being called a rascal.

Maeve often spoke to the creatures of the forest this way, for their presence soothed her, reminding her that she was not entirely alone. "I suppose ye're hungry, too," she murmured to the bird, plucking a juicy berry from her pouch. She tossed it upward and the raven caught it in its beak, gulping it down. "Plenty more where that came from," Maeve assured the bird, feeling a sense of satisfaction at providing for another—even if only in such a small way.

The feathery creature cawed as if in thanks before taking flight again, its wings sweeping through the misty air.

Maeve watched it disappear into the trees, and a pang of envy pierced her chest. The raven lived as part of a flock. It was never isolated as she was, cut off from her own kind. What would it be like to have someone to talk to, to confide in? Someone who knew her secret yet accepted her still?

Shaking her head, Maeve dismissed the fanciful thoughts. After all, such dreams were dangerous. She had learned long ago that she was meant to live apart. That her destiny lay far away from those of other people. Though she dared seek them out when trading fruits of the forest for a new blade or a piece of linen to fashion a new dress or cloak, she never risked lingering too long near villages or even small settlements.

Hoisting her satchel of berries, Maeve continued onward, wondering about this new stretch of forest, fresh ground beneath her feet. For fear of discovery, she never stayed in one place for too long, worried a hunter or traveler of some sort might come upon her by accident. Especially when caught off guard, Maeve knew that her curse often revealed itself.

And she could not risk that.

Rolling her shoulders against the heavy weight of the pack on her back, Maeve had only gone a few paces when a snapping branch stopped her short. She froze instantly, her body tensing. Had the mysterious man from before found her trail? Was he perhaps following her?

Although a rational corner of her mind argued that it could not possibly be so, that no one in these parts had ever laid eyes on her, Maeve still felt every inch of her begin to tremble. Her limbs grew weak, and she held her breath as she peered through the trees, trying to glimpse what had caused the noise.

There, just up ahead, a figure moved through the mist—tall and broad-shouldered. A man indeed. The same man as before. His dark hair fell into his face as he moved with slow steps, a heavy cloak draped upon his shoulders and a fierce-looking blade at his belt.

Heart pounding, Maeve backed away slowly. *Run!* It was like a scream inside her head, and Maeve flinched. All of a sudden, the pack on her back felt too heavy, its weight dragging her down as her limbs began to tremble in earnest. She knew she ought to flee, yet she could not seem to bring herself to move. Memories returned with full force, and panic and pain clawed at her heart. Dimly, she felt the straps of her pack slide from her shoulders and into the soft cover of leaves upon the ground. Her hand clasped a low-hanging branch, her fingernails digging into its bark as she fought to remain upright, fought to banish the memories that suddenly resurfaced. *Run!*

As though someone had shouted that word straight into her ear, Maeve flinched... and the man spun around and looked directly at her.

Their eyes met through the thicket of brambles, twigs, and leaves, and even through the haze, Maeve could see the man's sharp grey gaze.

A hunter! The voice screamed, and Maeve's pulse hitched. *Run!*

Chapter Two

A NEW LAIRD

Ewan MacDrummond kneeled by the babbling stream, cupping the crisp water in his hands. The chill bit into his skin, grounding him in the moment. He splashed his face, wiping away the sheen of sweat from his brow. The walk through the misty glen had been a welcome respite from the chaos back at the keep. Here, surrounded by ancient oaks and the rolling hills, he could pretend the immense weight on his shoulders did not exist.

A raven's caw drew his gaze upward. The sleek bird perched on a branch, sharp eyes studying him. Ewan's mouth quirked. "Fancy seeing ye here, friend," he exclaimed, feeling a certain sense of camaraderie to the creature. "It seems we both needed some time away."

The raven ruffled its inky feathers before launching into the air, and Ewan watched it soar, a pang of envy hitting him. How simple the life of a bird, able to roam wherever it pleased. No burdens, no expectations, no legacies to uphold.

With a sigh, Ewan rose, brushing the leaves from his plaid. He knew he could not linger here much longer. Soon Cromartie would send out a search party, furious at his disappearance.

Ewan smirked, picturing the dour man's tomato-red face. Aye, his father's old advisor meant well, and yet Ewan could not help but needle the man, even if it was childish. After all, Cromartie took himself far too seriously, his expression always earnest, always full of concern. Ewan could not remember ever having seen the man smile, his thoughts were constantly revolving around clan matters, around the future and how best to ensure it. It was a noble sentiment, to be certain; yet Ewan wondered if the man even knew how to live. Truly live. Or was this perhaps the essential piece of the puzzle Ewan could not quite seem to grasp? As laird of a clan, even one who had only just reached his twenty-second year, was he not supposed to have a life?

As Ewan meandered through the trees, the ancient pines creaked in the breeze. It was a soothing sound, familiar as a lullaby. How he wished to lose himself in this forest and leave the world behind. But he had made an oath, sworn on his father's deathbed to protect the clan no matter the cost.

The memory tightened Ewan's chest, and for a brief moment, he closed his eyes, remembering that dark moment barely a fortnight ago. Always had his father been like a force of nature, his voice booming across the great hall, his fist tight around the hilt of his sword, his eyes seeing, aware of everything that happened within his clan. He had been a great leader, devoted to his people.

Devoted to his son as well.

And now, he was gone…

… and Ewan was the new laird…

… responsible for his people.

Ewan sighed, his boots crunching on the needled ground. He knew he ought to return and face his duties. As much as he dreaded the negotiations with Lord Rutherford, he needed to prepare; he knew so even without his late father's advisor reminding him day in and out. Indeed, Ewan knew that he fell far short of his father's capabilities. He was still young and inexperienced, a burden that rested upon his shoulder's day and night. He had not expected to lose his father so soon, to be forced into the role of laird before he felt ready.

Now, though, the time had come whether he liked it or not, and he had made his father a promise. Still, deep down, Ewan wondered if he would be able to keep it or if he would let down his entire clan, unable to protect them from the English. Aye, his father had warned Ewan to be wary of the English lord, a distant relative on his mother's side. "Rutherford's a sly fox," he had croaked, his voice barely audible as his weak hand had clutched Ewan's arm. "He'll try to trick ye into an unfair bargain. Hold yer ground and keep the interests of our people first in yer mind."

A heavy sigh drifted from Ewan's lips. If only the matter could be solved with a clash of swords instead of words. Ewan smiled ruefully, his hand drifting to the hilt of his blade. He felt far more comfortable wielding steel than navigating tricky negotiations.

A sudden crack of a branch stopped him in his tracks, and Ewan's head snapped up, his hand flying to the hilt of his sword. His eyes scanned the misty trees, heart pounding. Had someone followed him from the keep? "Who goes there?" he called out sharply. "Show yerself!"

Only silence answered, and in that moment, the forest seemed almost devoid of life as though the whole world were holding its breath. After a tense moment, a red squirrel scampered up a nearby oak, disappearing into the branches.

Ewan slowly relaxed his grip on his sword, chuckling ruefully to himself. Likely just a deer or some other woodland creature startled by his approach. Still, the sound had put him on edge. He would need to be more alert here on the outskirts of MacDrummond land. Dangers lurked in the shadows...

As much as Ewan wished for it to be otherwise, he knew that he was not the only one who had doubts about his leadership abilities. While his late father's advisor had upon occasion remarked that Ewan ought to prepare himself most vigilantly for the days ahead, he had never quite stated his doubts with regards to Ewan's abilities. Neither had other clansmen. Still, Ewan could see the doubt in their eyes. He felt his father's seasoned warriors watching him, assessing him, judging him. They, too, felt unsettled by this sudden disruption of clan life. Always had they had faith in their leader. Always had they been secure in the knowledge that he would look after them and ensure their safety. Now, that certainty was gone. And no matter how far Ewan wandered, or how long he lingered, his responsibilities would remain. An entire clan depended on him now to lead and protect them.

Hanging his head, Ewan paused beside a moss-covered boulder before his gaze drifted upward to the shards of blue sky visible through the canopy overhead. He wished his father were still here. The great Laird MacDrummond had made it look so easy, commanding respect from both allies and enemies. Ewan was still earning the trust of the clan elders, still struggling to fill his father's boots. Would he ever succeed? Or was this an endeavor doomed to fail?

With one last sweeping look around, Ewan continued on, his senses heightened. He was laird now. Constant vigilance was required. His clan depended on it.

As Ewan walked on through the misty forest, the soft sounds of leaves and twigs crunching under his boots were soothing, and he felt his body relax even though his thoughts once more turned to Lord Rutherford's impending visit.

Beware the silver tongue of that sly old fox.

Aye, Rutherford was a cunning man, skilled at twisting words and obscuring meanings to his advantage. Though Ewan had only met the man once, he remembered his commanding authority, the way his sharp eyes took in everyone and everything, always assessing, always contemplating. Ewan would need to be direct yet tactful, strong yet diplomatic. It would be a delicate dance, a game of wits and will, with the stakes unbelievably high—and if he failed...

Ewan sighed, once again glancing up at the slices of blue sky visible through the canopy of trees. He wished his father were still here to guide him. The old laird would have known exactly how to handle Rutherford. Ewan still had much to learn when it came to clever negotiations and political maneuverings. He was more comfortable with a sword in his hand, solving disputes the old-fashioned way.

Only those days were fading. Words and parchment held more power now between the clans and the English lords who sought to control them. Ewan would need to adapt or risk falling behind, putting his people in jeopardy.

For their sake, he could not fail.

Weighted down by his brooding thoughts, Ewan continued along the wooded path. He knew Cromartie would be furious when he returned to the keep, for he had no doubt that the old advisor expected him to be preparing for their meeting with Rutherford, reviewing ledgers and documents.

Instead, here he was, wandering the forest to clear his head, shirking his responsibilities. He could almost hear Cromartie's irritated huff, see his bushy eyebrows drawing together as he launched into yet another lecture. "Ye're the MacDrummond now, laddie. 'Tis time ye started acting like it."

A twig snapped, and the sound ricocheted through the quiet forest. Ewan spun on his heel, hand flying to the hilt of his sword.

There, through a copse of trees, a flash of wild auburn hair and piercing green eyes met his gaze.

A lass.

Ewan froze, surprise rooting him to the spot as he stared at her. She stood motionless, staring at him as if transfixed, almost a mirror image of himself. Aye, he had not expected to encounter anyone out here, let alone a mysterious lass in the depths of the forest.

Despite her heavy cloak, she appeared young, near his own age. Her simple dress looked worn, and her boots were scuffed while her wild auburn hair danced on the soft breeze and her green eyes shimmered like emeralds against her pale skin. Aye, she was a sight to behold, and yet Ewan did not recognize her, certain he would have remembered her had their paths ever crossed. Then who was she? If she was not of his clan, where had she come from?

Endless moments passed as they looked at one another, and Ewan felt an odd pull, a strange sense of connection as he gazed into her eyes. If only he knew who she was. She seemed afraid, like a wild doe poised for flight, and yet, in her eyes, he did not see mindless panic. What he saw was rather a mind briefly frozen in shock but mere moments away from once again resuming its task.

Slowly, Ewan raised his hands to show he meant no harm. Then he took a step forward, gently pushing aside the branches that hung in his way. "Dunna be frightened, lass. I willna hurt ye." His voice was gentle, soothing.

At his movement, though, she startled, then quick as a fox she whirled around and darted away, disappearing into the trees as swiftly as though she were a wood sprite enveloped back into the shadows of the forest.

For a startled second, Ewan stared after her, his heart pounding, urging him to move. He did not wish to frighten her, and yet he had to know who she was. Aye, the thought of seeing her vanish, to never cross his path again, brought a sudden pain to his chest he could not explain. It was almost as though... he had been meant to find her this day?

Without another thought, Ewan rushed after her, his steps swift on the mossy forest floor, his gaze fixed up ahead on the soft swirl of skirts he glimpsed in between the trees.

The Highlands were a vast place, and yet the settlements were far and few in between. Was she perhaps a peasant girl from some nearby farm? Had she merely been startled to see the new laird out for a walk? Or was she a stranger, after all? New to these parts? Whatever the answer, Ewan knew he would forever regret it if he were to let her slip away. The green of her eyes—like the mossy stones in the burn—were filled with a deep sadness that called to him, and he rushed to catch up to her, knowing he could not fail.

Not in this.

Chapter Three

TWO STRANGERS

Maeve's heart pounded in her chest as she stumbled through the forest, her breath coming in ragged gasps. Her auburn hair clung to her sweat-streaked face while her eyes darted around, searching for a way out of this seemingly endless maze of trees and shadows, as the echo of footsteps thundered behind her. She knew she could not stop, the threat close upon her heels drawing ever closer still with each moment of hesitation. But where was she to go?

"Curse these blasted tree roots," Maeve muttered under her breath, narrowly avoiding another trip as she pushed herself to keep running. Her vision blurred, and she felt the constant need to look over her shoulder, to ascertain how far away her pursuer was. Was he gaining ground? Ought she perhaps rather hide somewhere instead of continuing to run? After all, she could not run forever. At some point, her limbs would give out and her breath would lodge in her throat. Indeed, with each step, her speed lessened, and whenever she glanced over her shoulder, the man's image drew closer. He was no longer a mere glimpse through the foliage, his large body slowly taking shape, his calls now echoing to her ears even though she could not make out the words he spoke.

With each pounding step, Maeve felt the gnawing fear of discovery grow stronger. She knew she had to find a safe haven, a place where she could catch her breath and gather her wits. And so, as she pushed through the last of the dense foliage, determination and fear fueling her every step, Maeve kept her eyes open for any sign of respite from her mad dash through the forest.

Despite the looming shadows and tangled roots that threatened to trip her at every turn, she felt a strange sense of kinship with this wild, untamed place—a bond that connected her to this place. After all, she had spent the past seven years living in forests, finding shelter under their canopy, and gathering food from what they provided. Truth be told, Maeve felt at home in this place, and the sense of fear that clawed at her heart as she suddenly found herself chased through this very place of peace and solitude threatened to trip her at each step. Was this truly happening? Though she had feared discovery these past years, she had never truly come close. Aye, she had kept her distance.

Always.

And she had been rewarded for it.

If only she knew what she had done wrong now. Had it been merely a coincidence for her to stumble upon this man here in these woods? Yet if he had not come to these parts to find her, why was he chasing her now?

The sound of footsteps echoed through the misty forest, their rhythm growing more insistent as they closed in on Maeve. Her heart pounded like a blacksmith's hammer against her ribs, each breath she drew coming in ragged gasps that did little to quell her mounting fear.

Who could this be? she wondered, her mind racing with thoughts of escape. *What does he want from me?*

"Stop!" a deep voice called out from behind her, its tone filled with authority. "Please! I swear I mean ye no harm."

Maeve did not dare heed his words. She did not even dare glance over her shoulder, now knowing he was so close. Fear lent her strength, even as her limbs trembled with exhaustion, she made to leap over a fallen log, desperate to escape.

Unfortunately, her foot caught on a protruding root, sending her sprawling face first into the damp earth. The taste of mud and moss filled her mouth, but there was no time for disgust or hesitation.

Scrambling back to her feet, she continued her desperate flight, driven by the relentless pursuit of her mysterious foe.

"Please," Maeve pleaded silently, her thoughts drifting to the ancient trees of these hallowed woods, wondering if some old power lingered within, a presence she had sometimes felt here and there. "Help me!"

"Enough of this foolishness!" the man behind her roared, his voice edged with frustration. "I mean ye no harm, lass! Ye have my word."

Maeve's panic-stricken mind refused to accept his words, her every instinct screaming at her to run faster, to flee from the unknown danger that stalked her through the shadowy depths of the forest. And yet, beneath the terror that threatened to consume her, a small spark of curiosity began to smolder.

Who is he? a part of her mind pondered, her eyes flicking back and forth as she sought any possible means of escape. *And why does he chase me so relentlessly?*

Only there was no time for answers, only action, her mind whirling with all that had happened and where it might lead. And then her thoughts stumbled over something, something recent, something she had not even noticed at the time and quite forgotten.

My pack!

As Maeve sprinted through the woods, she suddenly remembered her pack slipping off her shoulders and falling to the ground, holding all her meager belongings. "Curses!" Maeve hissed under her breath, the thought of losing everything she owned threatening to overshadow the fear of the man chasing her; she knew she would have to find it again.

Later.

When she was safe.

If she was safe.

The pounding of her heart seemed to match the quickening pace of her feet as Maeve burst from the forest and found herself at the edge of a river. The waters were rushing and churning, swollen by recent rainfall, and she hesitated for a moment, knowing the crossing would be treacherous. Her mind raced with thoughts of what might happen should she lose her footing, but as her pursuer's footsteps grew louder, she knew there was no time to find a safe away around.

"Please, let me make it across." Maeve could feel her heart thumping in her chest as her eyes darted back toward the forest and she saw the man emerge from the trees. He was tall and broad-shouldered, with long black hair pulled back in a tight braid. He wore a simple grey tunic and trousers, with a red and blue plaid swung over his shoulders. At his belt hung a long sword that glinted in the sunlight, his powerful arms and legs speaking of strength, of someone who knew how to fight.

With a deep breath, Maeve prepared to step into the current, her resolve hardening despite her lingering doubts.

"Wait!" the man called out from behind her, his breath, too, coming fast after the chase. "I'm not here to harm ye. I swear it!" A touch of frustration rang in his voice.

Maeve's heart twisted with conflicting emotions—fear, curiosity, and a desperate need to get away and save herself warred within her. Yet there was no time to consider, to ponder what to do. In a mere few seconds, he would bridge what little distance remained between them and reach her side, and then the choice would be taken out of her hands.

Steeling herself, Maeve plunged into the icy waters, her body felt briefly as though paralyzed from the cold and adrenaline coursing through her veins. Then the shivers began, and yet she waded deeper into the river, knowing she could not turn back.

"God's teeth!" the man swore from the shore of the river.

Cold water surged around Maeve's legs as she waded deeper into the river, the frigid liquid seeping through her clothing and making her tremble violently. Each step she took was a battle against the current, her soaked garments growing heavier by the minute. She could hear her pursuer's voice calling out to her, his words muffled by the relentless rush of water.

"Ye needa fear me!" he shouted, desperation clear in his tone. "I only want to help ye!"

Maeve gritted her teeth, trying to block out his voice as she focused on putting one foot in front of the other. The rocky riverbed shifted beneath her boots, making it difficult to keep her balance. Her heart pounded with mounting dread as she realized how precarious her situation had become. She could only hope that the man would consider following her too dangerous and thus abandon his pursuit.

As Maeve fought to maintain her footing, her thoughts raced like the water around her. She could not shake the feeling that she had made a terrible mistake, but the thought of coming face-to-face with the stranger frightened her even more than the river. If only there was some way to escape without endangering herself...

Desperation clawed at her chest as she pressed on, determined to distance herself from this man. Her thoughts were a chaotic whirl as she fought to keep her wits about her, cursing herself for her foolishness yet again. She knew she was risking everything, but in that moment, it felt like the only choice she could make.

Despite the sun's warmth upon her shoulders, the icy waters chilled her body until her muscles struggled to comply, aching with the effort of resisting the river's pull, each step forward feeling like a monumental task. Her soaked skirts clung to her legs, hindering her progress, and adding to her mounting frustration.

As the current surged around her, Maeve felt a sudden, bone-chilling dread claw at her chest, and for a brief, heart-stopping moment, her foot slipped on the slick riverbed, and she was pulled beneath the surface.

The world above disappeared, replaced by an all-consuming darkness that muffled her cries and threatened to crush her beneath its weight. Struggling against the oppressive force of the water, Maeve's lungs burned for air as her senses were overwhelmed by the cold, relentless rush of the current. Panic bubbled within her, threatening to consume her entirely. She could feel the icy tendrils of fear wrap around her heart, squeezing tighter with each passing second.

In the depths of her despair, Maeve suddenly felt a powerful warmth enveloping her. Strong arms wrapped around her waist, and she was pulled upward with an incredible force. The darkness that had threatened to consume her began to fade, replaced by a glimmer of hope as she broke through the water's surface.

"Ye're all right, lass," the man reassured her between gasps of air, his voice strained from exertion. "I've got ye."

Maeve clung to him, both grateful for her rescue and ashamed that she had allowed herself to fall into such a predicament. She could feel his heart pounding against her own, their breaths mingling in the cold air as he lifted her into his arms and carried her back toward shore, his steps more sure-footed than her own.

Hanging rather limply in his embrace, Maeve's mind raced with thoughts of escape, yet her body refused to comply, weakened by her struggle against the raging current.

Still, there was this other part of her that did not truly wish to escape. As embarrassed as she felt to even admit so to herself, Maeve could not deny that despite the chill it felt... wonderful to be held in another's arms.

There was warmth there, care and comfort, and a part of her wished she could remain precisely where she was. "Thank ye," she whispered, her voice cracking with emotion as she glanced up at the stoic-looking man carrying her to shore. "I dunna ken what would have happened if ye hadna come." She swallowed hard, still feeling the echoes of the fear that had gripped her heart so mercilessly the moment her head had gone beneath the surface.

And then the man lowered his head and his gaze found hers.

Maeve almost gasped. His eyes were a most unusual color. Not quite brown or blue, but rather something in between, something light and yet dark, something that glowed and glistened and at the same time seemed soothing and warm.

Water dripped from the loose strands of his black hair, and although his eyes never left hers, he kept on walking until they reached the shore. There, he settled her upon the soft grass, his warm embrace falling away as he sat back upon his heels. "Are ye all right?" he asked, his voice urgent and yet gentle. There was no more frustration or anger, nothing hard or threatening. "Are ye hurt?"

Swallowing hard, Maeve shook her head, her voice stolen from her throat. She stared at the man across from her, barely an arm's length away, and in that moment, she suddenly realized that his thoughts were no more than a distant hum. Despite their closeness, despite the fact that she could reach out and cup her hand to his cheek, his thoughts failed to manifest to a thundering roar inside her head. Why was that?

Over the past few years, thoughts of another—whenever she had happened upon another soul by accident—had pushed open the door to her mind with frightening force, invading without any thoughts or consideration for her. She had been helpless at their onslaught, always desperate to turn and run from them.

Now, though, it was as though the man's thoughts waited patiently outside her door. She could sense their nearness, hear their soft hum, and yet they waited and waited until she would open the door and grant them access.

It was the strangest sensation, and Maeve did not know what to make of it.

The man shook water from his hair, his eyes never leaving hers. "Who are ye, lass? Ye're not a MacDrummond, are ye?"

Again, Maeve managed a short shake of her head. She clasped her hands together, staring at the man across from her, waiting... for something to happen.

For his thoughts to attack.

Yet they did not.

"My name is Ewan," the man offered, his gray hawk-like eyes seeking hers, trying to look closer as though to unearth a secret that had been plaguing him for countless years. "Will ye tell me yers?"

Tears collected in Maeve's eyes, for she could not recall a single moment when another had looked at her the way this man—Ewan—was right now. She saw kindness in his eyes and curiosity, and for a moment, she thought that he was as desperate for company, for another soul to relate to, as she was herself. Yet how could she know? After all, she had yet to hear a single thought that coursed through his mind.

"Maeve," she whispered then, her voice barely audible above the roar of the river.

Still, Ewan smiled. "Maeve," he repeated, nodding his head to her in greeting. "'Tis a pleasure."

Maeve's heart opened in that moment. Aye, a pleasure, one she would never have expected.

Chapter Four

A GOOD PLACE TO HIDE

As the sun shone warm overhead, Ewan seated himself beside Maeve at the river's shore, the sound of the roaring water still ever present in his ears. Her auburn hair clung to her cheeks in wet tendrils, shimmering faintly in the light that glistened upon the water's surface. Her striking green eyes, wide with apprehension, mirrored the wild beauty of the ancient woods around them, and Ewan felt himself become quite entranced.

He all but forgot the sorry state of their dripping-wet clothing, the way the chilling autumn wind rustled through the leaves overhead. It was almost as though a water sprite had stepped from the river. One look into her eyes bewitched his mind and made him forget the man he was and the troubles of his days.

"Forgive me," Ewan said earnestly, his breath ragged from the chase. "I didna mean to frighten ye. I was just..." He paused, struggling to find the right words to express his concern without revealing his inexplicable fascination with this mysterious lass. "I was worried for yer safety. 'Tis not often that I come across someone in these woods. Let alone a lass. Let alone all by herself." He paused, wondering if she would volunteer an answer, any sort of explanation.

She did not. She merely sat upon the shore, her legs now drawn up and her arms wrapped around them, and stared at him rather warily. There was something bold and daring in her green eyes, revealing her as someone who had seen the world in all its facets, not merely the good and pleasant. Aye, there was pain there and regret, and yet Ewan saw a deep pool of strength, and in that moment, he knew her to be a survivor. Whatever had happened in her life, somehow...

... she was still here.

Despite the weight of her past experiences etched on her delicate features, her gaze flickered with curiosity between him and the dark forest beyond, as though she were deciding whether or not to trust this stranger before her.

"Where do ye come from?" Ewan asked gently, for he could not shake the feeling that there was something extraordinary about her, some hidden secret he yearned to uncover.

Instantly, her demeanor changed, became guarded. Then, she slowly shook her head, her hands tightening upon her arms. "I'd rather not say," Maeve replied with a somewhat defiant lift of her chin. Her voice, though, was barely audible above the rushing of the river.

Ewan nodded in understanding, and yet her reluctance to answer only added to the enigma that surrounded her, and he felt a sudden, irresistible urge to protect her. "Are ye alone?" he asked softly, concern furrowing his brow.

For a moment, Maeve hesitated, her gaze meeting his as though she were listening, waiting to hear a reply. Then, though, she blinked and gave a slight nod, and the vulnerability in her eyes touched Ewan's compassionate heart. He knew in that moment that he could not simply leave her here, cold and wet, in the unforgiving embrace of the forest. "Please let me help ye," he implored, his voice filled with sincerity. "I can offer ye shelter and warmth."

Maeve's eyes held a storm of emotions: fear, curiosity, and a yearning for connection that warred with her innate caution. Ewan sensed that there was so much more to this lass than met the eye, and he wanted nothing more than to unravel the mystery that she presented. He wanted... her here with him.

"Thank ye," Maeve whispered, her voice trembling like the leaves quivering in the wind. "But I canna accept yer offer."

Ewan's heart ached at her refusal, and for a moment, as they sat together upon the sun-soaked shore, the burden of being laird seemed to lighten, replaced by the simple human desire to connect with another soul. "Are ye often here in these woods?" Ewan asked, not quite knowing what to say, only certain that he wished to know more.

Maeve shrugged, and for a moment, her gaze swept over their surroundings, as though she had quite forgotten where she was. "I like the forest," she finally volunteered with a shy smile, her gaze once more trained upon his, as though she were waiting for something, almost as though she were straining her ears to listen. Perhaps it was simply the loud rushing of the river nearby that made her worry she would not catch his reply. "'Tis peaceful and kind." A shadow passed over her face, and Ewan felt his heart clench inside his chest. Aye, as young that she was, this lass knew pain.

And loneliness.

Perhaps it was that which made him reluctant to leave her side, which made him want to keep her close.

Ewan regarded her carefully. "Ye prefer the company of trees and birds," he murmured, not needing to make it a question because he already knew the answer. "Are people not to yer liking?"

Maeve tensed, as though she feared her answer would displease him.

Smiling at her, Ewan held up a hand. "I quite agree. I must admit. People often have a tendency to... intrude, do they not?" He held her gaze and saw that she understood, yet there was surprise in her gaze that he understood, that there was something they had in common. "I often come here," Ewan went on, wondering if she would reciprocate if he shared something of himself with her. "'Tis a good place to think, to be alone with one's thoughts." He chuckled. "'Tis a good place to hide if one doesna wish to be found."

A lighthearted chuckle fell from her lips, and in that moment, Ewan wondered if perhaps this was her true self. Had she been forced to hide it for so long that she barely recognized it now? Indeed, there was a flash of surprise in her eyes, and she clamped a hand over her lips as though she had long ago been forbidden to laugh.

For a long moment, they simply sat in silence. Then, Maeve spoke.

"Who do ye wish to hide from?" Her words came out slow, as though she were savoring each one.

Ewan sighed, leaning back upon his arms as his gaze swept out over the river. "Everyone," he finally replied, remembering the eyes that followed him wherever he went. "I am to step into my father's footsteps now that he's gone, and..." He shook his head and then sought her gaze, surprising himself. "I dunna think I can do it, and everyone agrees. Only no one has the courage to say so to my face."

Speaking these words felt strangely liberating, as though giving them voice had somehow taken a bit of their power. Still, it was the way Maeve looked back at him, so thoughtful, so understanding, that eased Ewan's heart. "Do ye ever feel like that? The need to escape from everyone around ye?"

At his question, Maeve bowed her head, resting her chin upon her bent legs. "Aye," she finally said, sadness gathering in her eyes. "People can be... difficult. 'Tis not easy to be around them if ye are... not what they want ye to be." Her gaze rose and met his. "I'd rather be alone than..."

Ewan nodded, wondering who it was people wished for her to be, who it was she could not be; yet he did not dare ask. "Do ye have a home?" he asked instead. "A place to stay?"

Again, Maeve hesitated, and when she finally spoke Ewan felt as though a great gift was being bestowed upon him. "I did. Once." Her mind drifted far away, her gaze suddenly distant. "Aye, I had a home. Long ago." She swallowed, and her eyes found his once more. "Now..." She shrugged then abruptly tensed. "Why did ye chase me?" Her eyes narrowed in suspicion.

"I..." Ewan knew that a wrong answer would once more send her fleeing his side. "I dunna quite ken. I heard a sound, and when I turned around, I saw... ye." He shrugged helplessly, unable to explain the sudden connection he had felt when their eyes had met. "When ye ran, I..." *I ken I couldna let ye slip away without knowing ye.*

The rushing river drowned out the wild hammering of his heart, his gaze fixed on hers and his breath lodged in his throat... until Maeve suddenly smiled.

Ewan could not say why. He did not understand, and yet somehow

Maeve understood what he had meant to say, though he had not been able to speak the words.

"It isna safe for ye to be out here alone," Ewan told her softly, glancing around the forest, considering all the dangers that might befall her out here, especially on her own. "Please, come back with me. At the MacDrummond keep, ye can warm up and dry yer clothes."

At his offer, her green eyes flashed with defiance and suspicion alike. "I dunna need yer help," she insisted, wrapping her arms around herself in a futile attempt to ward off the cold. She was clearly afraid, but her fear only seemed to strengthen her resolve. "I can manage on my own."

"Ye dunna have to, though," Ewan replied gently, leaning closer. He longed to know what secrets lay behind those guarded eyes, what experiences had taught her to be so cautious of others. "I promise I dunna mean ye any harm. Can ye trust that?"

Maeve hesitated, her gaze flickering away from him as if she were weighing the risks of admitting such a thing. Finally, she shook her head, her breaths shallow and quick. "Nay," she murmured, her voice tinged with regret. "I canna trust anyone, Ewan. Not even ye."

Although Ewan understood that he was no more than a stranger to her, regret still filled his heart. He sat back and raked a hand through his wet hair when, out of the corner of his eyes, he suddenly noticed her teeth chattering from the cold. "Please," he implored, his voice thick with emotion. "Let me help ye."

Determinedly, Maeve shook her head. "Ye've already helped me more than ye ken," Maeve whispered, her eyes welling up with unshed tears. "But I must be on my own now."

Her words of farewell stirred his heart, and his gaze flew around the forest floor, finally settling on a small stack of dry branches protected beneath a massive oak tree. "At least, let me make ye a fire," he exclaimed the moment he jumped to his feet and then rushed over to the massive oak. There, he kneeled down and collected them with urgency, his heart pounding in his chest as if it sought to escape and comfort Maeve itself. He knew that his actions were futile because the fire would only provide temporary reprieve from the cold. But he had to try.

Though clearly reluctant, Maeve nodded, and together, they settled beneath the oak tree.

With practiced movements, Ewan built a small fire, securing the site with rocks collected from the river's shore. Soon, the flames flickered and danced, casting shadows upon Maeve's delicate features. Her green eyes reflected the firelight as she leaned forward to warm her hands.

"Thank ye," she whispered, moving ever closer to the warmth. Despite the heat radiating from the fire, she still wrapped her arms tightly around herself, as though protecting her very soul from view.

"Ye're welcome," Ewan replied, his eyes never leaving her face. The sight of her shivering form tugged at his heartstrings, urging him to act. "Maeve, I canna bear to see ye suffering like this."

Maeve shook her head vehemently, her auburn curls dancing in the wind. "I told ye, Ewan, I canna go with ye. I must stay here." She met his gaze, and something that might be meant as a reassuring smile touched her lips. "Dunna worry. I've survived this long on my own," she assured him, her voice surprisingly steady despite the tremors that wracked her body. "I will be well."

"Promise me we'll meet again," Ewan begged, the words tumbling out before he could stop them. The thought of never seeing Maeve again was unbearable, and he desperately needed some reassurance that she would not vanish like a specter in the night. "Here, tomorrow at noon?"

Ewan was certain that she would refuse him, the expression in her eyes one of fear and caution. Still, she seemed to consider his request most carefully, as though a part of her truly wished to see him again, longed for his company as much as he longed for hers. And then, finally, after a small eternity, she spoke the words he had hoped to hear. "Aye, here at noon."

Ewan nodded, his hands curling into fists at his sides as he fought the urge to stay, to wrap his arms around Maeve and shield her from the world. But he knew his duty, and with a final, lingering glance, he rose to his feet, turned, and disappeared into the forest.

As he walked, his thoughts were consumed by Maeve, her every movement etched into his mind like a precious work of art. He could still feel the warmth of her body despite the shivers that had shaken her when he had carried her from the river, the way her breath hitched when he spoke her name. And as the burden of being a laird momentarily slipped from his shoulders, he allowed himself to imagine a world where they could be together, unshackled by the chains of duty and fear.

"Tomorrow," he whispered to the wind, a promise borne on the breeze that carried him forward into the unknown. "Tomorrow, I will ken ye better, Maeve. And mayhap, we shall find our way through this darkness together."

And for a moment, beneath the sheltering canopy of trees and the watchful gaze of the setting sun, Ewan MacDrummond allowed himself to dream.

Chapter Five

THE DANGER OF HOPE

Maeve stumbled back into her makeshift camp, her heart still pounding from her ordeal in the river. The night air clung to her damp clothes like a shroud as she shivered violently, her teeth chattering uncontrollably. In one hand, she held her heavy pack while the other clutched a torch, which she had lit from the fire Ewan had made for her before extinguishing it. Its dancing flames cast eerie shadows on the surrounding trees as she made her way back to the small hidden clearing where she had slept the past few nights. She had meant to be on her way; now, though, it was already too late in the day for traveling even if she were not soaked to her skin.

After changing into the one spare dress she possessed, Maeve warmed herself by the fire she had made from the torch, and her thoughts turned to Ewan—as much as she tried to redirect them, certain they would cause her more harm than good. Still, her heart and mind were unrelenting, conjuring Ewan's image and the way he had looked at her as he pulled her from the river. Aye, there was no denying that she had been drawn to him, his grey eyes filled with concern and kindness. But even as gladness blossomed within her, caution tempered the feeling. She could not forget the danger others posed to her well-being, her life even, the secrets she kept buried deep inside a chasm that could not be overcome.

Maeve knew it to be true, had learned this lesson the hard way and knew she would be a fool to disregard it.

"Och, why did he have to find me?" Maeve muttered to herself, her fingers playing absently at the frayed edges of her shawl. The truth was that she longed for companionship, for the comfort of another's presence. It had been so long since anyone had come close, had embraced her, or even simply looked at her with something akin to affection or concern. For a long time now, Maeve thought the memory of such a connection had all but slipped from her mind. Perhaps with time people grew accustomed to anything and the loss they had suffered would no longer pain them. Now, though, after the moment she had shared with Ewan, Maeve knew different.

As content as she had convinced herself to be before, now, she could no longer believe her own lie. When his eyes had met hers, something had stirred back to life inside of her, a deep yearning for closeness, for the simple comfort of a touch. There was something about Ewan MacDrummond that beckoned her, a sense of belonging and safety that she had not felt in years.

At the same time, though, fear clung to her like a second skin, reminding her of the potential consequences should her secret be revealed. *What would I do?*

Maeve shook her head as if trying to dislodge the thoughts that swirled within it. "I canna let myself be drawn in," she whispered, her eyes glistening with unshed tears. "'Twould only bring ruin to us both."

But even as she uttered the words, Maeve found her gaze drifting in the direction of the river and a fierce longing surged through her, a desire to know Ewan better. Deep down, she knew she ought not, yet she also knew that she would never forget the look in his eyes when he had rescued her from the river, the way he had held her close as if she were something precious and fragile. "Damn ye, Ewan MacDrummond," Maeve muttered under her breath, a wry smile tugging at the corners of her mouth. "Why did ye have to be so bloody kind?"

Wrapping her arms around herself, Maeve shivered, feeling the chill in the night air. Yet it was not merely the cold that trailed across her skin, raising goosebumps. Still, she scooted closer to the fire, listening to its soft crackling sound, its sparks illuminating the darkness in a dance of light and shadow. Conflicting emotions surged through her heart—relief that she had been saved, gratitude for Ewan's kindness, and the undeniable longing for companionship she had felt around him.

"Confound it all," Maeve whispered, her breath visible in the frosty air, as she stared into the dancing flames and suddenly found herself grappling with a mystery she could not quite fathom: why had Ewan's thoughts not overwhelmed her like others before?

Staring into the flames, Maeve allowed her mind to travel backward, recalling the moment she had first sensed Ewan in the forest. Aye, in that moment, she had felt the usual onslaught of another's thoughts, and she had shied away from it. Yet later, by the river, everything had been different.

Running her fingers through her damp hair, Maeve bit her lower lip, recalling the way Ewan had looked into her eyes, the way he had held her safely cradled in his arms as he had carried her to shore. She had been overwhelmed and terrified from her experience in the icy river, her mind focused elsewhere. Had that been it?

Maeve buried her face in her hands, her body once more wracked with shivers despite the warmth from the dancing flames. "His presence... 'twas different," she stammered, her teeth now chattering uncontrollably. "I even spoke to him." Her eyes stared into the dark beyond, and yet in her mind's eye, she saw the moment by the river once more. "I spoke to him, and it felt..." Indeed, his thoughts had been there; Maeve had sensed them. Yet they had not attacked her. Why? Was there perhaps something unusual about him? Was it possible that he, too, possessed some sort of... power?

"Or was it me?" Maeve whispered into the stillness of the night. Aye, that second time, *she* had felt different, her mind focused elsewhere, not for a moment contemplating Ewan's closeness, not for a moment expecting to be overwhelmed by his thoughts. Had that been it? Was there perhaps a way for her to keep the door to her mind firmly locked, to keep others out?

Never had Maeve considered such an option, and she suddenly felt foolish. Had there been an answer to her problem all along and she had simply not seen it? Was there perhaps a chance for her to live among people after all? The notion intrigued her but also filled her with trepidation. What if she took this risk and Ewan discovered her ability? Would he see her as a monster, or worse, a threat to be eliminated?

As she contemplated the potential consequences of meeting Ewan the next day, Maeve paced back and forth, her steps leaving imprints on the soft earth. The thought of allowing him into her carefully guarded world sent shivers down her spine that had nothing to do with the cold. And yet, the alternative—fleeing once more, abandoning the fragile connection they had forged—was equally unbearable.

Her heart wavered between hope and fear, torn between the desire for a life beyond her lonely existence and the terror of being discovered. As the night wore on, Maeve's thoughts tumbled, her mind a battleground where love, regret, and sacrifice waged war beneath the watchful gaze of the ancient Scottish stars.

Chapter Six

TWO LOST SOULS

Dawn broke over the Scottish Highlands, casting a golden glow on the dew-covered heather. Ewan MacDrummond awoke with a feeling of eagerness stirring within him, a sensation he had not felt in years. He could hardly wait to see Maeve again—her auburn hair and striking green eyes haunted his thoughts.

"Enough o' this idleness," he muttered as he swung his legs over the side of his bed, his grey eyes alight with determination. Dressing hastily, Ewan ignored the clan matters awaiting his attention and instead set off into the woods early, his every footfall echoing with purpose.

As he journeyed deeper into the forest, his mind wandered back to their encounter by the river. The image of Maeve's trembling form, her fear mixed with defiance, fueled his resolve to find her. There was something about her that called to him, something beyond her beauty and mysterious charm. It was a connection he could not quite grasp, but one he knew he must explore further.

Yet as Ewan reached the riverbank, he found it deserted. The early morning sun glistened upon the waters, and birds trilled in the trees. Ewan stood in the very spot where they had spoken the day before, his gaze turning every which way, his heart occasionally pausing in his chest as he waited to glimpse her come toward him from between the trees.

Hours passed, though, without any sign from her, and Ewan soon found himself unable to remain where he was. Large strides carried him back into the woods, his eyes scanning in all directions, his heart now tense in his chest as fear slowly trailed down his spine. *What if she doesna come? Ye arrived early. Yet now 'tis noon, surely.*

Aye, Maeve had been reluctant the day before. There had been caution, fear even, in her green eyes, now making Ewan wonder if she had perhaps left in the night, desperate to escape another meeting with him. Had he been so mistaken? Aye, he had sensed her unease, her wariness, and yet for a moment, he had felt something between them. He had seen her smile. He had seen her green eyes darken with emotion as they had looked into his, and in that moment, he had been certain that she, too, had felt something as they had sat side by side by the river.

Ewan stilled as the soft scent of smoke drifted toward him. He breathed in deeply, and his eyes caught a flash of movement beyond the thicket that barred his way.

Finding his way around, he stumbled upon a small hidden clearing containing a makeshift camp. At its center stood an unassuming lean-to, constructed of branches and foliage and a small fire pit lay nearby.

And there, still asleep in the small shelter was Maeve.

"Ye've been living in these woods all this time?" Ewan whispered as he slowly stepped toward her, his gaze fixed upon her face, pale beneath the vibrant hue of her auburn hair. A mixture of admiration and concern filled his chest at the sight of her, and his heart ached at the thought of Maeve surviving alone, exposed to the elements and danger.

Lost in the sight of her, Ewan paid no attention to his surroundings, and his booted foot stepped on a small twig. The crack echoed across the small clearing like a gunshot.

In an instant, Maeve shot upward, her eyes wide as she swept them around her surroundings, fear visible in her tense muscles, her right hand clutching a small dagger.

Ewan exhaled a slow breath at seeing her thus, and he vowed

quietly to himself that he would protect this woman who had captured his heart and stirred his very soul so completely. "'Tis me," he said softly, stepping toward her, his hands raised in reassurance. "I'm sorry. I didna mean to startle ye."

The moment Maeve beheld him, a deep breath rushed from her lungs and she closed her eyes, all terror falling from her. "Oh, 'tis ye." She wiped a hand over her eyes, then she blinked and looked at him again. "What are ye doing here?" She frowned then slowly scrambled to her feet, pulling a heavy cloak tighter around her shoulders.

Ewan could not help the sheepish grin that came to his face as he shrugged. "I came to meet ye, and when I found our spot by the river deserted..." He shrugged again.

For a moment, Maeve stared at him, clearly caught off guard by something he had said. "Our spot?" Her words were no more than a whisper, and yet they made Ewan realize the meaning behind what he had said. Aye, he had revealed more than he had wanted.

More than he had been aware of.

Ewan cleared his throat. "Do ye... Do ye live here?" The question slipped from his lips before he could stop it, its answer self-evident.

Maeve wrapped her arms around herself, her eyes now downcast. "We all do what we must," she mumbled quietly before lifting her gaze once more and meeting his eyes. "Ye ken nothing about my life."

Ewan nodded. "Ye're right. I dunna... but I wish to." He took a step toward her, her eyes wide and watchful. "Please, come with me."

She flinched as though he had struck her. "Come with ye?" She shook her head and backed away. "I canna!" Fear now lingered in her eyes, and yet Ewan thought to see something else as well, and he responded to it without thinking.

"I willna leave these woods without ye, lass," he said gently, not wishing to frighten her. Yet he knew he had to stand his ground if he wished to keep her in his life. "Ye're not safe here, and there is a better place for ye."

A disbelieving chuckle left her lips—quite against her will it would seem, for she clamped a hand over her mouth a moment later.

"I mean what I say," Ewan replied to her silent reaction. "I wish to look after ye, Maeve." He swept his gaze over her makeshift camp. "Will ye tell me what brought ye out here?"

For a moment, her eyes widened before she shook her head in refusal.

Ewan could not deny that he was disappointed, his heart longing to know this elusive woman. "Verra well," he finally said. "I willna press ye. Yet I willna be able to sleep a wink in the nights to come if ye stay out here by yerself." He cast her a tentative smile then held out a hand to her. "Please. There's room for ye at MacDrummond Castle. Ye'll be safe there. I promise."

Her mouth opened as though she wished to answer, yet no sound fell from her lips, her green eyes wide with fear... but also temptation.

"Ye'll be safe at Castle MacDrummond, I promise," Ewan insisted once more, his eyes filled with determination and sincerity. He took a step closer, reaching out to gently grasp her trembling hand. "I will protect ye, Maeve, from whatever lives in yer past. Ye're no longer alone."

"Ye dunna understand," Maeve whispered then, her voice cracking under the weight of her emotions. Tears pooled in her eyes, threatening to overflow. "'Tis not safe for me among people. I..."

Ewan frowned, uncertain what it was that she feared. "I promise that no harm will come to ye," he vowed, holding her chilled hands tightly within his own. "My people are kind and devoted to one another, and I have nay doubt that they will welcome ye." Ewan's voice was gentle but firm, his eyes locked on hers, searching for understanding.

"Ye swear ye'll protect me?" Maeve asked unexpectedly, doubt in her eyes as though she sought to expose him as a liar.

"By all the gods and Old Ones, I swear it," Ewan vowed, his voice strong and unwavering. "I will let nay harm come to ye, Maeve, on my honor as laird of Clan MacDrummond."

Her eyes flew open, and Ewan realized that she had not known of his position among his clan. "Ye're the laird?" She looked him up and down, and a frown came to her face.

Ewan swallowed hard. "Aye, I am. My father... just passed on." His gaze fell from hers, and he inhaled a deep breath, remembering the life he had sought to escape the day before when his feet had guided him into the woods. Aye, he had barely thought of the burden of filling his father's shoes these past few hours, his mind solely occupied by the young lass across from him now.

"I'm sorry," Maeve whispered, and when Ewan looked up, he saw her move toward him. Her green eyes were filled with sadness and loss, and he could all but feel her reaching out to him, offering comfort. Within the blink of an eye, their roles had reversed. Before, he had been the one to offer comfort and safety, and now, her hand squeezed his. "How did it happen?"

Ewan stared at her, his limbs suddenly cold. Indeed, they felt frozen in place, as though no matter how hard he might try, he would never be able to move them again. "A fever," he muttered, surprised that his lips moved and words fell from his tongue. "A sudden... chill." He shrugged, disbelief sweeping through him like a tidal wave. "He was always strong, always there, always..." Maeve's image blurred as tears filled his eyes.

"Ye havena grieved him yet," Maeve murmured, the slight frown upon her face voicing her surprise. "Why not?"

Ewan closed his eyes, suddenly overwhelmed by something he had not seen coming. And then, he felt Maeve's touch, her small, chilled hand against his cheek and his heart filled with grief. Grief not for the chieftain whose shoes he would never fill, but instead, grief for the father who had loved him and watched over him every day of his life.

Fueled by an almost desperate need, Ewan wrapped Maeve in his arms, not because he wished to reassure her or even because he longed to feel her in his arms. Nay, in that moment, he needed her. He needed her strength and her kindness as much as he needed her familiarity with loss and grief. And she did know; Ewan was certain of it. He felt it in the way she responded to him, resting her head against his shoulder, and slinking her arms around his middle, holding on tightly. She spoke not another word but simply held him close, sharing his grief in a way no one else had since his father's passing.

Yet her body trembled against his own, and Ewan knew how much courage it had taken for her to take this step toward him. Aye, she had been alone most of her life. He knew this by the way she looked at him and held herself separate, unaccustomed to other people standing close. Still, she had not hesitated to offer comfort when he had needed her and the thought warmed his heart. "Will ye come with me?" Ewan murmured into her hair, unable to imagine another day without this woman by his side. He had only met her the day before, yet it had changed him just like his father's passing.

For a long moment, Maeve said not a word. Then, a heavy breath fell from her lips and her arms tightening around him as though for courage. "Aye, I will."

"Thank ye, lass," Ewan breathed, relief washing over him as they stood there together, amidst the quiet beauty of the forest.

Chapter Seven

WELCOME TO MACDRUMMOND CASTLE

The first glimpse of Castle MacDrummond sent Maeve's heart racing, her pulse pounding in her ears as she clutched Ewan's arm tighter. It was as if the very walls were crafted from the mountains themselves, standing strong against the relentless winds that buffeted the Highlands. The imposing presence of the wary soldiers guarding its entrance only added to the sense of foreboding that settled within her chest.

Perhaps it had been a mistake to have kept herself apart from people for this long. Of course, Maeve had had good reason to do so. After everything that had happened, it had been the only choice. Still, now, she began to doubt whether she had truly thought everything through at the time. Indeed, in retrospect, Maeve realized that she had acted out of fear alone.

Her gaze swept over the tall castle walls, and she imagined all the people within, the distant echo of their voices teasing her ears. She could sense their thoughts just the same, close by, not far, drifting toward her, pulling her in. Instinctively, Maeve shied away, her steps retreating, her hand still clutched upon Ewan's arm. It had become second nature to her to flee, and yet Maeve managed to call herself to reason.

Inhaling a deep breath, she looked up into Ewan's eyes, needing something, anything to ground her.

"I'm here with ye," Ewan murmured gently, seeking to reassure her, as though he knew precisely what she needed. Yet, his gray eyes were slightly narrowed in confusion, for he could not possibly understand what frightened her. Nevertheless, he saw her fear and sought to alleviate it.

Maeve nodded, hearing his words, even more than that, hearing his kindness and compassion. She felt his thoughts nearby, swirling around her, asking to be heard. Yet they were no threat. Not anymore. For some reason, they were no more than an option, not something forced on her.

Maeve also sensed the thoughts of others nearby; although these felt more persistent, she did not feel the same terror she had before. Aye, something had changed. Perhaps it had simply been her fear that had given the thoughts of others more strength, more power. Perhaps she had been utterly wrong to run from them, to curse them, to see them as something that was done to her. "Perhaps I can do this," she murmured more to herself than anyone else. "Perhaps I can walk among people again."

Hope blossomed in her heart as she turned her gaze to Ewan, his gray eyes shining with utter joy, as though her peace of mind meant everything to him. "Ye're strong," he murmured, his tone still gentle and encouraging. "I canna rightly say that I ken what ye've been through, but ye have the look of one who kens how to survive." His warm hand clasped hers, a silent promise. "Perhaps now, 'tis time to move past merely surviving, Maeve." A rather enchanting smile came to his face as he shifted closer, his gaze never leaving hers. "Perhaps 'tis time to live again."

Maeve nodded, astounded by his words. Of course, her own mumbled utterances had done little to explain her past, her fear. Yet somehow, Ewan understood the pain she had known. Aye, she wanted to live again, and not merely survive from day-to-day. Perhaps, he wanted the same.

The day before, when he had spoken of his father, Maeve had glimpsed a very vulnerable side to this tall dark warrior, laird of his clan, and it had been surprisingly simple to respond to it. She had felt drawn in, her instincts, long buried, reawakening and taking over, guiding her down a path she had never thought she would ever find again.

Compassion.

Aye, to feel with another, to have someone understand; those were truly precious moments of the human experience, were they not?

"Welcome to Castle MacDrummond," Ewan whispered, his warm breathing teasing the shell of her ear as he leaned close to her. His voice was a warm embrace in the chilling air, and where a moment ago Maeve had felt uncertain, questioning whether she had made the right choice in coming here, she suddenly felt hopeful. Of course, she had been overwhelmed by the idea of leaving her solitary existence behind, for it had been all she had known for so long. Now, though, the constant fear she experienced every day was tempered by something most unexpected: hope that something other than loneliness awaited her upon the horizon.

"Ye've not been around people in a long time, have ye?" Ewan murmured as they stood side by side, her hand still clamped upon his arm, his own still covering hers, keeping her safe. "We ken very little about one another." He sighed, seeking her gaze. "How could it be any different? Yet... there's a part of me that feels as though... I ken ye, as though ye ken me."

Maeve's breath lodged in her throat as she looked into his eyes and felt his words reach out to her. "Aye, I feel it as well. 'Tis why I'm here."

Another one of those enchanting smiles graced Ewan's features, speaking of such utter joy that Maeve felt momentarily overwhelmed, the corners of her own mouth twitching as though wishing to reciprocate. "Ye'll not leave my side?" she whispered, trying her best to ignore the armed warriors standing guard upon the parapets.

Slowly, Ewan shook his head from side to side. "Not unless ye give me leave to do so," he proclaimed, a most earnest expression in his eyes as though he had just sworn an oath. "Ye'll be safe here. I promise."

Maeve nodded in agreement. "Let us go inside then," she

murmured, her voice wavering, her nerves aflutter. Still, if not now, when?

As they approached the castle gates, Maeve could not help but notice the wary gazes of the men stationed there, their guarded expressions betraying a deep-rooted suspicion toward strangers. She swallowed hard, reminding herself that she was no longer alone—Ewan was by her side.

The clang of iron against iron echoed through the air as the portcullis was raised, granting them entry into the castle courtyard. Maeve walked beside Ewan on wobbling legs, heavily leaning upon his arm, her eyes wide as they drifted from face-to-face, the hum of thoughts growing louder.

"Welcome home, Laird MacDrummond," one of the guards greeted Ewan, who nodded in response, his hand squeezing hers reassuringly.

"Thank ye, Donald," he replied, before turning to Maeve with a small smile. "Come, let me show ye inside."

As they crossed the threshold, Maeve could feel the curious stares of the clan members upon her, their whispers floating through the air like the rustle of leaves in the wind. She knew they were wondering who she was and why she had arrived at their laird's side, aware that her presence was shrouded in mystery and intrigue. But for all their curiosity, there was a certain wariness in their gazes, too—she was an outsider, and the Highlands were not known for their hospitality toward strangers.

"Who is she?" one woman murmured to her companion as Maeve passed by, her eyes meeting Maeve's briefly before flitting away.

"An English lass, perhaps? A gift from Lord Rutherford?" a young man suggested with a snicker, only to be silenced by a sharp elbow to his ribs.

"Have ye no manners?" the older woman by his side scolded, her cheeks flushed with embarrassment. "She can hear ye, ye ken."

Maeve kept her gaze lowered, her heart pounding against her ribcage as she followed Ewan deeper into the castle. Despite the hope that had taken root in her heart, she felt exposed, vulnerable beneath all those prying eyes. It was only Ewan's reassuring warmth that steadied her, reminding her that she was not alone in this strange new world.

"Pay them no heed," he murmured, his voice low and soothing. "They're merely curious, that's all. And they'll come to see that ye're no threat, soon enough."

Maeve nodded, pressing her lips together as she fought against the dizzying cacophony of thoughts that buzzed around her like a swarm of angry bees. She closed her eyes for a brief moment and took a deep breath, willing herself to remain calm, to not allow the thoughts of others to overwhelm her. And so, she focused her mind and heart on Ewan, on the man by her side, and slowly, bit by bit, the ruckus echoing to her ears calmed.

Cleared.

Suddenly, she could make out individual thoughts here and there, not clearly, not with precision or understanding. Yet as they walked up the large staircase to the next floor, their footsteps echoing along, Maeve realized that not all the thoughts she heard, full of questions and doubt, were directed at her. Indeed, quite a few were directed at the man by her side.

At Ewan.

And it sent a cold chill down her back.

Chapter Eight

A SAFE PLACE

Ewan felt Maeve's fingers dig into his arm with a strength he would not have thought she possessed. He sensed her tension, her unease, saw the way her eyes flitted from side to side, a cringing expression coming to her face every now and then. It was as though something assailed her, attacked her, something sharp and painful, there one moment and then gone the next.

Though Ewan wished to ask, he knew that Maeve was not yet ready for his questions. He needed to give her time or she would run from him, and he could not risk that.

"Are ye all right, Maeve?" he asked gently, his gaze seeking hers as they navigated the dimly lit corridors of the castle.

"Aye," she replied, forcing a smile onto her face that spoke of courage, of determination. Clearly, despite whatever fear lived in her heart, she wanted to be here; and it made Ewan hope. "I'm only... a wee bit overwhelmed, is all."

"Understandable," Ewan acknowledged with a reassuring nod. "This place can be quite daunting, especially when ye're new. But I promise, it'll start to feel like home soon enough." He could only hope so, for what if it did not?

Holding onto her, he led Maeve through a heavy wooden door, and they stepped into a cozy chamber with a large four-poster bed and a small writing desk that sat by the window, which offered a breathtaking view of the loch in the distance. "Ye'll feel at home here soon," Ewan murmured again, hoping that saying so out loud would make it so.

Then he squeezed her hands and released them before quick strides carried him to the fireplace, where he stacked a few logs and then lit them. The faint crackling of the small fire echoed through the chamber, its flames dancing tentatively, casting shadows upon the stone walls as the autumn sun in the distance slowly began to set.

As Ewan once more turned to look at Maeve, her eyes were wide yet not with fear.

With awe.

"Do ye like it?" Ewan asked, gesturing around the room, touched by the shimmer of tears he saw in her eyes. "I hope I..." He stepped toward her and grasped her hands, waiting until her eyes focused upon his. "If there is anything ye require, ye only need ask."

Blinking back tears, Maeve nodded, her voice thick with emotion as she took in the welcoming chamber. "Thank ye, Ewan. 'Tis beautiful."

Utterly relieved, Ewan smiled. "Good. Ye deserve to feel comfortable here, Maeve." He squeezed her hands, suddenly surprised how natural it felt to touch her like this, to hold her hands within his own despite the short time they had known one another, even though they were little more than strangers who had met only the day before.

Indeed, that moment by the river felt as though it had happened lifetimes ago.

"Thank ye," Maeve repeated, her gratitude genuine as she glanced around the chamber once more. Then her eyes locked with Ewan's, and he could see how vulnerable she felt. "I must admit, I still feel a bit nervous about all this." Her lower lip trembled ever so slightly.

Ewan nodded in understanding. "That was to be expected, was it not? Ye've taken a big step today, and I'm proud of yer courage."

A faint flush graced her cheeks, and she briefly averted her gaze in a way that made Ewan wonder if no one had ever spoken to her like this.

"Will ye be all right by yerself for a little while?" he asked cautiously, sensing her immediate unease. "I willna be far, and I willna be long. I promise ye'll be safe here." He smiled at her. "No one will bother ye. I'll make certain of that."

Lifting her chin, Maeve nodded. "Aye, I shall be fine."

"I shall be back shortly to fetch ye for supper," Ewan told her, his hands still holding onto hers. "I simply wish to inform those closest to me of yer arrival, for I hope that it shall smooth things a little."

Again, Maeve nodded, and for a moment, Ewan thought that a part of her regretted coming here. Aye, it had been a big step, and he could only imagine what it felt like to be suddenly thrust into a world so unlike the one she had known. Though he could not be certain, he would guess that she had spent the past few years of her young life living all by herself out in the woods. How that had happened, he could not say; but he wished that one day she would share her story with him.

Ewan made to step away when he suddenly paused, overcome by a sudden longing. His hands moved to grasp her face, gently, tentatively, and then he leaned down and placed a tender kiss upon her forehead. "I'll return soon," he whispered, her green eyes wide as they looked up into his. "I'll not be long."

Her breath trembled as she nodded, her right hand moving to cover his, still cupped to her cheek. "Will ye kiss me?"

Her words caught Ewan off guard. Of course, he had wanted to steal a kiss. He had wanted to from the very moment he had laid eyes on her. Yet he had been afraid to take advantage, knowing how vulnerable she was. Still, he had been unable to stop himself from reaching for her and placing at least a tender, chaste kiss upon her forehead. "Are ye certain?" Ewan murmured, his head already leaning down to hers. "Ye owe me nothing. Yer staying here isna dependent on—"

"I ken. I wouldna be here if I thought otherwise," Maeve assured him in a voice that suddenly rang strong and with certainty. A small smile teased her lips, and something almost wicked sparkled in her green eyes. "'Twas merely a request; one ye're free to refuse, of course."

Ewan chuckled, and his gaze strayed to her lips. "I wouldna dream of it." He lowered his head another fraction, feeling her breath tease his lips.

"I'm glad to hear it," Maeve murmured, and as she spoke the last word, her mouth brushed against his, his arms pulling her deeper into his embrace.

Ewan felt this kiss in every fiber of his being. He felt calm and excited all at the same time, eager and at peace. He kissed her gently, savoring each moment, each touch and puff of breath against his lips. He felt the tips of her fingers trace along his skin, down the side of his face until they slowly curled into the collar of his shirt, as though she wished to bind them together for all the time to come.

At her silent declaration, Ewan almost lost himself, swept away by something he had not expected to find these days. His heart had been so burdened, so heavy, that this sudden sense of lightness was beyond precious. "Ye're a rare lass," Ewan murmured against her lips. "I canna believe I found ye. I canna help but think that I was meant to."

Maeve chuckled, a light, almost carefree sound. "I canna believe a lot of things." Her green eyes looked into his. "But ye feel quite real." She touched her hand to his cheek then suddenly gave him a pinch. "Aye, ye're real."

Ewan laughed then stepped back. "Go rest," he told her, giving her hands one last squeeze before he moved toward the door. "Supper will be served soon, and I will come back to fetch ye."

Maeve nodded, and Ewan forced himself to step across the threshold, to tear his eyes away and eventually, after another long, lingering look, to close the door behind himself. Then he pushed all thoughts of Maeve away as he went in search of Cromartie and Aunt Innes. He could only hope supper would go well.

Chapter Nine
AT SUPPER

The great hall of Castle MacDrummond was bathed in an amber glow, the light of countless candles flickering upon the high, vaulted ceiling. The long wooden tables were laden with sumptuous fare, and Maeve breathed in the savory scent of roasted venison and plump pheasant, bowls of steaming vegetables, and thick slabs of fresh bread. Her hand once more rested upon Ewan's arm as they stood in the arched doorway, listening to laughter and conversation, voices echoing through the air as the clan gathered for their evening meal.

Yet despite the warmth and camaraderie around her, Maeve felt a chill run down her spine. She glanced nervously at Ewan, who stood by her side, his hand resting reassuringly on the small of her back. His presence was a comfort, but it could not entirely dispel the unease that tightened in her chest like a coil. As they made their way to their seats at the head of the table, she could sense the curious eyes of the clan members upon her, their whispers fluttering through her mind like so many restless birds.

"Ye'll be fine," Ewan murmured, giving her a gentle smile as he pulled out her chair. "I'll not leave ye, aye?"

Maeve nodded, doing her best to shut out the thoughts of those around her as she sat down, the weight of their curiosity bearing down upon her like a heavy cloak.

Directly to her right sat an elderly woman, formidable in her bearing with hawk-like eyes and, Maeve presumed, a sharp tongue. "May I introduce my late father's sister, Innes MacDrummond," Ewan intoned, his right hand coming to rest upon her shoulder. "Aunt Innes, this is Maeve. She is... a dear friend." He glanced down at her and smiled, and despite the chill in the air, it warmed Maeve's heart to have him stand at her side.

"'Tis a pleasure to meet ye," Maeve said kindly, despite the buffeting thoughts that wished to storm her mind, thoughts she suspected belonged to Ewan's aunt—judging from the intense look in her eyes.

"And this," Ewan continued, nodding to his other side where an elder man with a rather serious countenance sat, his keen eyes regarding her shrewdly, "is my trusted advisor, Cromartie."

Nods of greeting were exchanged before everyone was seated and supper began. Maeve felt herself the object of many curious glances from Ewan's clan, and she tried to lose herself in the tastes and smells of the food before her, savoring each bite as if it might somehow anchor her to this moment, to this place. Yet as the meal progressed, she could not shake the feeling that she was being watched by someone in particular.

"So, lass," Aunt Innes said abruptly, leaning forward with a predatory grin, "Ewan has told us precious little about ye. Where do ye hail from?"

Maeve swallowed hard. "From the Lowlands, ma'am," she replied carefully, her voice steady despite the pounding of her heart. She glanced at Ewan, who cast a warning look at his aunt.

Aunt Innes, however, disregarded it without a second thought. "Ah, the Lowlands," she mused as she rolled her eyes in a mocking gesture. "Aye, I've heard of that place."

The woman on Aunt Innes's other side laughed but stopped abruptly when Aunt Innes sent her a scathing look.

Maeve suppressed a chuckle, suddenly intrigued with Ewan's aunt.

"Were ye not the one who always reminded me to show good

manners?" Ewan remarked in that moment as he leaned toward his aunt, his hand settling on Maeve's in reassurance. "Especially when speaking to guests?"

His aunt regarded him for a moment then nodded. "I apologize, dear. Well, ye hail from the Lowlands. Where then?"

At an encouraging nod from Ewan, Maeve shrugged. "Here and there," she replied truthfully. "I've never quite had a home, not like this." She swept her gaze over the gathered clan in the great hall, their voices mingling in camaraderie. "Ye're blessed to find yerself a part of something so wonderful."

Aunt Innes's eyes narrowed, and Maeve thought to see a touch of approval in the old woman's eyes. "Aye, I suppose I am." After that, she said not another word, and yet her thoughts swirled wildly and more than once Maeve was tempted to open the door and let them in, to hear what it was the other woman was thinking. Was she suspicious? Or merely curious? Not knowing felt like an itch Maeve barely resisted scratching.

He's a fool! The thought suddenly burst into Maeve's mind like a roar in her ear. She could not quite say where it had come from, yet she knew that it was filled with anger. *He will doom us all.*

A cold shiver snaked down Maeve's back as she turned her gaze to Ewan, suddenly certain that the thought she had overheard had been about him.

"Are ye all right?" Ewan asked as he leaned closer. "Do ye wish to retire?"

And who is that woman? He doesna truly intend to make a stranger mistress of our clan, does he? He isna that much of a fool!

Maeve's head whipped around, and her eyes scanned the assembled clans people. While many glanced in her direction, most seemed engaged in conversation, laughing and jesting. Then, though, she found a pair of eyes that drilled into her, seething with anger. "Who is that man?" Maeve whispered to Ewan. "The one over there who keeps staring at me."

Ewan exhaled a slow breath, and Maeve knew that whoever the man was had already given Ewan reason for concern. "His name is Drystan. He served my father loyally for decades."

Ewan did not say more, and yet Maeve knew that this could not be the end of the story. Was it possible that this had something to do with the doubts and uncertainties that had drifted into her mind ever since arriving at the castle? Aye, from what little she knew, it seemed that Ewan's father had passed away recently, passing the lairdship to his son, and while most saw it as a natural occurrence, some held concern for the future of the clan, not trusting in Ewan's ability to see them safe. Clearly, Drystan was one of these men, and now, by coming here, Maeve had strengthened his disdain for Ewan.

"Ewan said he all but stumbled upon ye in the woods," Aunt Innes remarked in that moment, drawing Maeve's thoughts back to the woman at her side. "How did that come to be?"

"Chance, I suppose," Maeve answered, her gaze flicking briefly to Ewan before returning to his aunt, as she forced her thoughts to focus on the conversation. "I met Ewan by happenstance, and he was kind enough to invite me to stay."

"Indeed?" Aunt Innes raised an eyebrow, her scrutiny unwavering. "And what of yer family? Surely, they must be missing ye?"

Maeve hesitated, her fingers tightening around her fork as she weighed her words. She did not wish to lie, and yet not even Ewan knew the full truth of her past. "I have no kin to speak of."

"Such a tragedy," Aunt Innes clucked, though her eyes were alight with curiosity. "To be so alone in the world... But fear not, lass, for ye are amongst friends here."

"Thank ye, ma'am," Maeve murmured, grateful for the reprieve, however temporary it might be.

Throughout the remainder of the meal, she did her best to focus on Ewan, allowing the warmth of his presence to chase away the shadows of doubt that threatened to engulf her whenever Aunt Innes dared ask another question or her eyes met Drystan's across the hall.

Eventually, though, the echoes of laughter and clattering cutlery began to fade as supper drew to a close. Maeve's eyes darted around the great hall, trying to avoid Drystan's suspicious glares that seemed to follow her every move. She sensed his distrust, and it made her heart race with anxiety. Yet Ewan's hand settled upon hers every so often, holding it gently within his own, entwining their fingers, so that

Maeve often forgot everything else around her, her thoughts consumed by the man at her side. Never had she experienced such a sense of belonging, which, of course, was not surprising considering how she had lived these past years. Still, it was all the more overwhelming, and Maeve felt herself teeter between caution and an almost overwhelming desire to simply throw herself into Ewan's arms and enjoy the sudden closeness.

"It has been a long day, has it not?" Ewan murmured in her ear, his warm breath teasing her skin. "Do ye wish to retire?" he asked as he had before.

Maeve smiled at him and nodded. "Aye, I do." Indeed, the thought of her chamber was a most pleasant one. Never had she had such a place all to herself with no one to intrude upon her, offering warmth and comfort.

Ewan rose to his feet and offered her his arm. "Allow me to escort ye."

Maeve loved this gallant side to him, the way he seemed to look out for her, always aware of her needs. "Thank ye." It made her feel special and wanted and... cherished. It almost made her feel loved, too.

As they ascended the stairs to her chamber, though, Maeve's thoughts raced. She could not shake the feeling that her arrival had complicated Ewan's position among his people. What if they were to discover her secret, would they cast her out? Would he? More than anything, Maeve wished Ewan already knew her past, for her greatest fear was that he would find out and then turn away her.

Her heart ached at the prospect, for she could not ignore the warmth that had blossomed within her ever since he had stepped into her life. She dreaded the thought of losing it, of losing him, seeing his eyes turn hard as he sent her away. Was this perhaps too great a risk? Perhaps not to her life but her heart?

With a deep breath, Maeve entered her chamber as Ewan held the door open for her, eager to find a measure of solace. The fire crackled softly in the hearth, casting a warm, flickering glow across the room, and for a moment, Maeve stared into the flames, her heart pounding and her breath coming in shallow gasps.

"Something upset ye, did it not?" Ewan asked softly as he closed the door behind him. His gray eyes held hers as he stepped forward, his steps cautious as though he were not certain about what to do.

Maeve heaved a deep sigh. "Yer people dunna want me here," she remarked straightforwardly, not wishing to add more lies and omissions to their relationship. "They wonder about me. No doubt they..." She could not quite finish the sentence, for it would suggest that somehow, she believed there to be a future for them. Would he laugh at the notion? Maeve could not believe it to be so, and yet she could not bring herself to speak her mind.

"Ye dinna needa worry, Maeve" Ewan said softly, reaching for her hand. "People are always wary of strangers. 'Tis in their nature to avoid the unknown, to protect themselves in the case of danger." His touch felt like a lifeline, grounding her, and offering a momentary reprieve from the concern that flared to life once again. "Were ye not also wary of me when we first met?" He grinned at her teasingly.

Maeve chuckled, knowing his words to be true. She looked into his grey eyes, searching for any sign of doubt or hesitation, but all she found was unwavering determination. "Aye, ye're not wrong. I was wary, but ye proved that I needna be."

Ewan nodded. "And they, too, will come to see the truly wonderful lass that ye are. Give them time, and they will lo—" He broke off abruptly and cleared his throat, a rather bashful expression upon his face.

Knowing what he would have said, understanding what that simple sentence reflected about himself, Maeve turned away, her hand slipping from his as her feet carried her closer to the warmth of the fire. She did not wish for distance, and yet she was afraid for hope to grow. Had it only been yesterday that their paths had first crossed? It seemed impossible.

"I'll let ye sleep now," Ewan whispered, his voice barely audible over the crackling fire. "'Tis been a long day."

Maeve turned to meet his eyes. "Aye, it has. Thank ye for... bringing me here, for being ye." He stepped toward her then, and his hand moved to cup her chin, raising her face to meet his gaze. "I never thought I'd ever..."

His other arm wrapped around her middle, pulling her closer, his gray eyes looking deep into hers. "I canna pretend to understand the burden ye carry, but I want ye to ken that I'm here fer ye, no matter what."

Maeve's heart swelled with gratitude, and she felt a warmth spreading through her chest that had nothing to do with the fire. For the first time since she had arrived at Castle MacDrummond, she allowed herself to believe that mayhap she could find a place here—a place where she could belong.

"Ye should try to rest now," Ewan urged gently, releasing her chin, and taking a step back. "We can talk more come morning."

"Aye, come morning," Maeve whispered, utterly entranced by these moments when she stood in Ewan's embrace. They made her feel invincible, deeply hopeful, and utterly... tempted.

Throwing caution to the wind, Maeve closed the remaining distance between them. Her hands slipped into Ewan's hair as she pulled him down to her, claiming his mouth in a deep kiss. Never had she felt such a powerful emotion before, but in this moment, she knew that she was safe with Ewan, as she allowed her body to melt into his embrace.

He returned her kiss eagerly, and his lips moved expertly against hers as if they had been made for each other. The kiss seemed to last an eternity, pushing away all her doubts and fears and leaving her feeling blissfully alive.

At least for one precious moment.

When at last their lips parted, Maeve closed her eyes, savoring the warmth of his presence. His hands moved slowly up and down her back in a comforting gesture as he rested his forehead against hers and they breathed the same air.

"Ye dunna needa fear," Ewan whispered softly into her ear, his words echoing through her mind and soul. "Ye belong here now."

Maeve gazed up at him through misty eyes, letting out a long sigh of contentment before nodding in agreement. She smiled softly and wrapped her arms around him again, wanting to remain in this moment forever, her heart filled with an unspoken understanding of what had just occurred between them—something special... something that could only be found in another's presence.

Chapter Ten

A GREAT MAN

Ewan knew that there were other matters that required his attention; still, the moment he woke, his thoughts strayed to Maeve, his limbs eager to carry him to her side once more. And thus, shortly after breaking their fast in the great hall, Ewan asked her to accompany him on a stroll through the forest. To his delight, Maeve accepted eagerly, her eyes shining at the prospect of leaving behind the castle and having a few precious moments to themselves.

As they walked out the castle gates, Ewan was aware of the whispers that followed them, and he worried—as so often—about the way his clan saw him now that he was their laird and no longer their laird's son. Aye, the responsibility resting upon his shoulders now was still an unfamiliar weight, and there were days when Ewan almost forgot the burden he now carried, awakening in the morning with the certain belief that life was still the same.

After all, he did not feel like their laird. It was a position that did not naturally come to him, and he knew that for him it would be a struggle day in and out to become the man he needed to be to fill his father's shoes.

Today, though, Ewan wished for nothing more than a reprieve, Maeve the only one who soothed his soul and eased his heart.

Together, they walked through the wild expanse of the Highland forest, their footsteps in sync as they were drawn deeper into the woods, farther away from the castle and its people. The scent of damp earth and verdant foliage hung heavily in the air while vibrant wildflowers painted splashes of color against a backdrop of emerald green. The soft murmur of a nearby stream wove its way through the trees, creating a melody that seemed to harmonize with the whispering breeze.

For a long time, no words passed between them, and yet it was a comfortable silence. Ewan felt himself breathe easily, his shoulders relaxing as he lifted his head and allowed his eyes to sweep over the sparkling foliage above.

"Tell me about yer father," Maeve said abruptly, her voice gentle yet probing. "What was he like? And what of yer mother?"

Ewan hesitated, surprised by her sudden question. He paused in his step, and his gaze sought hers, emotions bubbling beneath the surface as memories of his father filled his mind. "I barely remember my mother," he admitted, feeling a deep sense of regret. "She died when I was verra young." He paused as the distant echo of laughter drifted to his ears from sometime in his past. "I remember them together. Not well, mind ye. But... they loved each other. 'Twas like the sun rose the moment their paths crossed, and the world seemed suddenly brighter. I dunna remember much about her, or them, but that stayed with me."

Maeve seemed almost entranced as she listened, and Ewan wondered about her own parents. Had she ever known love? Seen it in them? Or experienced it herself? As young as she was, had there ever been a man in her life?

"My father," Ewan continued quickly, feeling his emotions revolt at the thought as he struggled to keep his voice calm, "he was a strong laird, well-respected by the clan." He sighed heavily, raking a hand through his hair. "He was a man who knew how to command loyalty. People had faith in him, and every day of my life, I saw their certainty that no matter what happened, he would bring everything to a good end." A slight tremble seized his shoulders, and he rolled them against the uncomfortable sensation. "He did his best to train me in his image, yet..."

Hanging his head, Ewan simply stood beneath the trees, his gaze distant as he remembered the man his father had been all his life. He remembered his kindness and his strength, the way he had always stood tall, proud, and certain. Always had he seemed like a hero of the ancient stories to Ewan, and now that he was gone, Ewan suddenly felt like a lad again, left outside in the cold.

Alone.

A soft touch upon his arm brought his mind abruptly back, and he almost flinched as his gaze moved to find Maeve standing right beside him. Her green eyes shimmered with tears, as though she had just read his thoughts and knew precisely the loss he felt, the sense of abandonment he could not seem to shake.

"Yer father was a great man," she said gently, her hand upon his arm tightening, holding on, pulling him closer. "Yet he wasna *born* a great man." Her green eyes looked deep into his. "He grew into the man he became, and like ye, he knew moments of uncertainty and doubt."

Ewan frowned. "How do ye ken?" Her words touched him, and he realized that he needed them to be true. Ever since his father's passing only a few short weeks ago, he had felt terribly inadequate, as though he had failed his clan already.

"Because everyone does," Maeve replied simply, such wisdom in her eyes that Ewan did not dare doubt her. "We all come into this world unprepared. We all learn and grow and are sometimes faced with... moments that seem too hard to bear." She swallowed hard, and for a second, a shadow danced across her features. "Yet we survive." She nodded along to her words, her gaze far away, as though she no longer spoke of him and his father but rather of herself. "Life changes who we are, who we used to be, and yet that is perhaps precisely what is meant to happen. It shapes us into the people we need to be to live in this world." A heavy sigh drifted from her lips.

Ewan watched her, wondering about the secrets she kept so close to her heart. "Ye speak as though ye ken this from experience," he murmured, placing a hand upon her shoulder.

A shiver went through her before she looked up and met his eyes. "Do not we all?"

Ewan nodded, seeing hesitation in her eyes, and he knew that she was not yet ready to confide in him. For a long time, their gazes held before she abruptly cleared her throat and took a step back. "I can only imagine the burden ye carry," she said softly, blinking her eyes rapidly as though to discourage tears. "But yer father must have trusted ye to bear it."

"Indeed," Ewan replied, his voice thick with emotion as he reached out to grasp her hand, pulling her back before she could slip away. Their eyes met once more, and she paused in her step. "Before he passed," he continued, not wishing for this moment to end, "he made me swear to protect our clan at all costs. 'Tis a promise I intend to keep, but sometimes... sometimes I canna help but wonder if I'm truly up to the task." Aye, it was a painful moment to be sure, to reveal all this about himself, to make himself so vulnerable, and yet it felt good to say these things out loud.

Maeve reached out with her other hand and touched his arm, her warmth seeping through his clothing and into his very being. "Ye are more than capable, Ewan MacDrummond. I can see it in yer eyes. Ye care about people. Ye truly care. Ye helped me even though I am no more than a stranger to ye." A sad smile graced her lips, and her eyes shimmered with tears. "Ye may not ken it yet, but ye will find yer path. Dunna try to walk yer father's. Ye canna be him, and ye are not meant to be him. Ye can only ever be yerself."

Ewan stared at her, completely overwhelmed by those few simple words. All this time, he had asked himself how to replace his father, how to become more like him, how to do the things he had done precisely like him. And now, here Maeve stood, insisting that he do not.

Still, her advice rang true, and Ewan could feel it echo through his bones.

"Tell me more about yer father, not as the laird, but as the man who raised ye," Maeve asked gently, her hand trailing down his arm, her touch sending shivers down his back.

Inhaling a fortifying breath, Ewan tried to focus his thoughts away from the tempting woman who stood so close that he could pull her into his arms in less than a heartbeat. Still, his very soul ached, and he knew that sharing his doubts and uncertainties with Maeve would ease the pain. "Father was... a strong man," he began, his thoughts drifting backward. "He was strict but fair. He had a way of making everyone feel important and valued. As a child, I idolized him." A wistful smile formed on his lips as he continued, "I remember how he used to tell me stories of our ancestors, their bravery in battle, and the importance of loyalty to our clan. Those tales inspired me, made me want to be like them, like him."

Maeve listened intently, her green eyes shimmering with empathy. "Yer bond must have been very deep. 'Tis clear that his influence remains with ye even now."

Ewan nodded, feeling a tightness in his chest as he spoke of his father. "We were close. His death... it left an emptiness inside me that I fear will... remain for the rest of my life." He paused, swallowing hard against the knot in his throat.

"Loss has a way of doing that," Maeve murmured, understanding etched across her features. "But it also allows us to grow, to learn from the pain and emerge stronger. Yer father would be proud of the man ye are, Ewan. I have no doubt that he *was* proud of ye. Even though ye might doubt yerself, I'm certain that he didna. He knew what it meant to be placed in this position. He knew 'twould take time for ye to find yer own way."

Again, Ewan found himself staring at her, awestruck by the insight she possessed. Her words were not spoken with hesitancy but with a certainty that stole the air from his lungs. "Thank ye, Maeve," he replied, almost breathless, deeply touched by her compassion. He looked into her eyes, seeing not only understanding but also a hint of shared sorrow. "Ye've known loss, too, have ye not?"

Maeve's eyes flickered with sadness, but she nodded. "Aye, I have. And like ye, I've had to find my own path forward."

"Yer strength is inspiring," Ewan admitted, his admiration for her growing with each passing moment. "There are no words to describe how grateful I am to have met ye." He reached out and cupped his hands to her face, his gaze holding hers. "The day I stumbled upon ye..." He shook his head ever so slightly, overwhelmed by the sudden thought that had he not gone out into the forest, their paths would never have crossed.

"I ken," Maeve said softly, her hand brushing against his. "I feel it is well, and I am equally caught off guard by it." A tear-heavy chuckle left her lips. "I am grateful as well because... I care for ye, Ewan." She closed her eyes and shook her head as though regretting what she had said. "I ken I shouldna, and yet..."

Their eyes locked, the bond between them strengthening with unspoken words as their hearts echoed the same sentiment. In that moment, they were united not only by their shared pain but also by a newfound trust and understanding, two souls drawn together by the inexorable pull of fate.

As they stood there, the gentle breeze caressed their skin, carrying with it the subtle scent of wildflowers. The world around them seemed to pause as if giving them the space to breathe and find solace in each other's presence. Ewan could not help but notice how the sun lit up Maeve's auburn hair like a fiery halo, making her green eyes sparkle with an ethereal glow.

Overwhelmed with gratitude for the unexplainable twists and turns of fate, he reached out and gently tucked a delicate wildflower behind her ear. It was a small gesture, yet one that spoke volumes about the blossoming affection between them.

Maeve's cheeks flushed with warmth, her eyes shining. "Thank ye, Ewan. I've never known anyone like ye, and I wish..."

Unable to resist the magnetic pull between them any longer, Ewan leaned in and captured Maeve's lips with his own. The kiss was tender yet passionate, an intimate dance of emotions that sent shivers down his spine. It felt as though a spark had ignited deep within his soul, binding them together in a way neither had ever experienced before.

Just as their lips began to part, the unmistakable sound of hurried footsteps echoed through the forest.

Startled, Ewan and Maeve broke apart, and he saw her spin away, turning her back as she struggled to regain her composure. Ewan turned around to see Cromartie approaching with quick strides, his expression tense and urgent.

"Forgive me for interrupting, my laird," he panted, clearly out of breath from his haste. "But ye must return to the castle immediately. There's been word."

Ewan's heart raced, his mind a whirlwind of thoughts as he tried to process the sudden intrusion on their intimate moment. Indeed, the expression upon Cromartie's face could only mean one thing: Rutherford was near.

"Verra well, Cromartie," Ewan replied, his voice steady despite the turmoil within. "Lead the way then." He offered Maeve his arm, and as they followed Cromartie back toward the castle, he could not help but steal a glance at her.

Their eyes locked for a brief moment, secrets shared and kept now hanging between them as well as an unspoken promise of trust and affection. Aye, she was the one, and Ewan suddenly knew the kind of man he wanted to be.

The man who conquered her heart.

Chapter Eleven

LORD RUTHERFORD ARRIVES

The wind whispered through the heather, carrying the sweet scent of blooming flowers as Maeve walked alongside Ewan, their footsteps quickened as they followed Cromartie back to the castle. The sun shone brightly upon the horizon, painting the sky with shades of gold and orange, a beautiful contrast to the somber mood that had settled upon them.

Although Maeve could open her mind to the thoughts of others, to know their emotions she had to rely on her other senses. Yet the tightening in Ewan's shoulders and the slightly twitching muscle in his jaw revealed only to easily that whatever message Cromartie was bringing could not be considered good news.

Maeve longed to ask, and yet the distant expression in Ewan's gaze told her that she could not be selfish in this moment. Clearly, he struggled with his next steps, considering what to do, and it would not do well for her to distract him.

Still, Maeve could not keep herself from gently squeezing his hand, reminding him that he was not alone, that she believed in him, that whatever he would have to face, he could.

At her offer of reassurance, Ewan glanced down at her, a soft smile gracing his lips and gratitude shining in his eyes.

Cromartie, ever vigilant, slowed his pace when he saw the silent communication between them until he was walking beside Ewan. His hardened features softened slightly with concern as he addressed his young laird. “My laird, our scouts have spotted Lord Rutherford’s party approaching.” His gaze flickered to Maeve, and she could see that he was displeased by her presence.

Ewan’s brow furrowed as he turned to Cromartie, the weight of his responsibilities settling on his broad shoulders. “How soon will they arrive?”

“By nightfall, my laird.” Cromartie paused before continuing, his gaze flicking toward Maeve yet again, clearly indicating that she had no place in the upcoming negotiations. “Ye need to prepare.”

“Thank ye, Cromartie,” Ewan said, nodding curtly. He glanced at Maeve, an apologetic expression crossing his face. “I’m sorry, lass, but I must attend to this.” His gaze swept over the castle gates with people bustling in and out. “I shall show ye to yer chamber first, though.”

Maeve smiled at him, touched by his thoughtfulness. Aye, he had vowed not to leave her side without her permission, and she knew he would never break his word.

“My laird. ’Tis of the utmost importance that we—”

Ewan lifted a hand to stop Cromartie’s objection. “And we shall,” he replied calmly, holding the older man’s gaze. “As soon as Maeve is settled safely in her chamber.”

“’Tis all right.” Grasping Ewan’s hand, Maeve met his eyes. “Go ahead. I shall be fine.”

A concerned frown came to his brows and he moved closer, his voice dropping to a whisper. “Are ye certain? Truly, ’tis no bother.”

Maeve nodded to him in encouragement, aware that Cromartie stood nearby, hanging on every spoken word. “I am. Go. See to yer people.” Perhaps it was wise to do her utmost to gain Cromartie’s trust. After all, the man did not strike her as hostile in any way, merely as someone concerned for his laird and his people.

“Verra well,” Ewan replied before he quickly cupped a hand to her cheek and then bent to place a kiss upon her forehead. It was an impulsive decision, done in the moment, and the second he stepped back, Maeve could see that he realized what he had done.

Aye, he had just now revealed to all those nearby that he cared for her.

"My laird?" Cromartie pressed, his gaze flickering back to the castle.

Ewan nodded and then turned away, giving Maeve's hand one last squeeze. "I shall see ye soon."

As Ewan and Cromartie hurried ahead, Maeve could not help but feel a pang of anger.

With fate.

With herself.

Even with Rutherford.

More than anything, she wished she could remain by Ewan's side to help him through this. He was a capable man, and all he needed was someone who believed in him. Maeve was certain that he would serve his clan well once he managed to shake that sense of uncertainty, of inadequacy. Yet would he be able to do so in time for the negotiations?

Gritting her teeth, Maeve watched Ewan and Cromartie step through the gates and into the courtyard, struggling to banish all thoughts of the negotiations from her mind. After all, what good would it do to worry? There was nothing she could do to help, only watch from a distance and hope for the best.

For the first time in Maeve's life, frustration gnawed at her insides as she watched Ewan's back stiffen, his fists clenching at his sides. She could sense the tension radiating from him like waves crashing against a storm-tossed shore, and then almost without conscious thought, she let her mind brush gently against his, allowing his thoughts to enter her own.

Even from a distance, his thoughts were clear, unclouded. *Lord Rutherford is shrewd and cunning*, Ewan's inner voice echoed in her head. *How do I meet him? What if I fail my people?*

Frozen in place, Maeve stared after Ewan, only now realizing what she had done.

Before, everything had been different. Before, she had not known that she could block other's thoughts from her mind. It was still a struggle, and yet especially in Ewan's presence it became easier with every moment that passed.

And now, she had intentionally violated his privacy, his innermost thoughts. If he knew, would he hate her for it? Could a man ever love a woman who possessed the ability to listen into his every thought, whenever she chose? Could he ever trust her enough not to do so without permission? And had she not just done exactly that, crossed that line without being invited in?

Maeve's eyes shimmered with unshed tears as she struggled with this decision, torn between honesty and the possibility of losing Ewan forever. She ought to tell him; she knew that. And yet, every fiber of her being revolted against it, terrified of the consequences.

As she lifted her gaze, her eyes collided with Drystan's. The man stood up high upon the castle walls, watching her, his gaze narrowed.

Maeve swallowed hard, feeling a slight tingle in the air as his thoughts drew closer. They stood right outside the door to her mind and all she needed to do was open it and allow them in, and then she would know what it was this man was thinking whenever he looked at her.

What was right and what was wrong? Maeve wondered in a way she never had before. As lonely as her existence had been, it had been simple. Now, she knew not quite which path to walk. Indeed, if it was wrong to use her ability ever—without permission!—then why did she have it in the first place? Did not all people use their abilities? Did not everyone possess something another did not?

Holding Drystan's distant gaze, Maeve lifted her chin, regarding the man shrewdly. Then she took a step forward and closed her eyes.

It canna possibly be a coincidence that she is here now, Drystan thought, anger lacing his words. *She arrived mere days before Rutherford. No doubt he sent her to spy on us, to gain information that would aid him. And the lad is falling for her female wiles. The fool! He will doom us all.*

Maeve stood there for a moment, the cold Scottish wind tugging at her auburn hair, before she turned away from Drystan and toward the castle, determination now etched into her mind. Aye, there was a way for her to help Ewan, even if it meant keeping her secret locked away in the depths of her heart. Perhaps, one day, their love could stand strong, unburdened by secrets and lies.

But not today.

Too much was at stake.

Maeve took a deep breath, and with each step she took toward the castle, her determination grew stronger. Aye, all it took was some practice for her to focus her ability and gather information to give Ewan the advantage he needed during the negotiations with Lord Rutherford. The thought brought a spark of hope to her heart, pushing back the shadows of doubt and fear that had been lurking there, and her steps quickened.

Inside the great hall, the tension hung heavy in the air like an unrelenting fog, as the clan members prepared for Lord Rutherford's imminent arrival. Whispers of worry and anticipation filled the space, as everyone feared the outcome of the negotiations.

Ken ye what this means? thought an elderly woman near the arched doorway to the great hall, her silent words gripping Maeve's mind tightly and jerking her to a halt. *If wee Ewan canna come to an agreement with the English lord, our people will suffer.*

Maeve sighed. *Wee Ewan?* Indeed, his people did think of him as a lad. Aye, he was young, certainly younger than most men when they stepped into their father's positions. Still, he possessed heart and strength and given time he would make them proud.

Unfortunately, there was no time. Would Ewan lose the respect of his people?

The thought pained Maeve, and she knew she had to find a way to support him. Yet even if she managed to unearth something helpful in Rutherford's mind, how could she let Ewan know without revealing her deepest secret?

As the hour approached, Maeve found herself pacing in the shadows of the great hall, desperately trying to hone her ability to gather any useful information. She focused her thoughts, channeling her senses inward until it felt like a burning fire, ready to be unleashed. "Focus, Maeve," she whispered under her breath. "Ye can do this."

The sound of hooves echoed in the distance, signaling Lord Rutherford's arrival, and the tension in the great hall reached its peak. The clan members fell silent, their eyes fixed on the entrance, their hearts no doubt thudding painfully in their chests.

The time has come, Maeve thought, steeling herself for the challenge ahead. She breathed in deeply, determined not to let her emotions overwhelm her, and carefully opened her mind to the thoughts of those around her.

As the doors swung open and Lord Rutherford strode in, followed by his entourage, Maeve felt a sudden surge of something... unexpected course through her. It was as if the very air crackled with energy, urging her to action, guiding her path.

Her thoughts.

Willing her body to relax, Maeve lifted her gaze and looked upon Rutherford. He wore fine clothing that spoke of wealth and status; velvet robes lined with fur and embroidered with intricate patterns woven from gold thread. His face was wrinkled and weathered, his grey hair cut short, framing a strong jawline that seemed to be set in stone when it came to negotiations. But despite all this finery, it was his piercing gaze that made people take notice whenever Rutherford entered a room; like an eagle surveying its prey before striking it down without mercy.

Indeed, his eyes were shrewd, clearly looking at Ewan as he stood at the hall's other end to unearth any sign of weakness, seeking every advantage that could be exploited to further his own goals.

"Welcome to Castle MacDrummond," Ewan greeted the clan's visitor from across the border, his voice steady despite the doubt Maeve knew lived in his heart.

Hiding in the shadows, Maeve kept her eyes focused upon the newcomer, ready to wield her ability to protect these people and the man she... had come to love.

Quite inexplicably.

And as the first words were spoken between Ewan and Lord Rutherford, the fate of Clan MacDrummond hung in the delicate balance, poised on the edge of a knife.

A balance Maeve hoped to tip in their favor.

Chapter Twelve

AN ENGLISHMAN & A SCOT

Ewan stood tall in the great hall of Castle MacDrummond, surrounded by his clans people who watched him with a mix of anticipation and concern. The weight of their expectations bore down on him like a thousand stones, each one heavier than the last. He could feel the cold draft that seeped in through the ancient stone walls, yet his palms were slick with sweat as he rubbed them nervously against the coarse fabric of his kilt.

Inwardly, Ewan battled with his own doubts about the upcoming negotiations with Lord Rutherford. His father had always been stalwart and decisive in such matters, but Ewan knew he did not possess the same natural authority. The thought of facing the cold, calculating English lord made Ewan's stomach churn, the bile rising in his throat as his thoughts strayed to the possible consequences.

Ewan—as well as every member of Clan MacDrummond—knew that the late laird had only entered into an agreement with an Englishman like Lord Rutherford out of need. After the Battle of Culloden, many Highland clans had been severely weakened, suffering starvation due to lack of resources. Therefore, in order to save his people, Ewan's father had made a deal with Lord Rutherford to provide food in exchange for future loyalty and service.

Aye, it was an awful deal, and Ewan remembered his father's tense face whenever he had spoken of it, for he had always feared for his people's future. The threat of his people being forced into service to an English lord, torn from their homeland to toil fields elsewhere, ripped from their families. Still, it had been the only way, and Ewan had been certain that when the time came, his father would find a way to protect their clan once more.

Now, his father was gone.

"Stand strong, my laird," whispered Cromartie, leaning in close to Ewan's ear. "Remember what yer father taught ye."

Ewan nodded at the old man's wise counsel, taking a deep breath to steady himself. He could almost hear his father's voice echoing through the hall, urging him to show no fear, to be the leader that the MacDrummond clan needed and deserved.

The heavy oak doors creaked open, and Lord Rutherford entered the great hall, followed by his entourage. His wrinkled face was marked with years of experience and hardship, and his sharp eyes exuded an air of disdain for Ewan and his kin. He strode forward with an air of arrogance, his velvet cloak billowing behind him like a dark cloud.

"Welcome to Castle MacDrummond," Ewan forced himself to say, doing his best to project a confident demeanor despite the unease gnawing at his insides. "We are honored by yer presence."

As the English lord approached the dais where Ewan stood, he felt the ghosts of his ancestors watching, urging him to stand firm and protect his people. He knew that this moment would define not only his own legacy but the fate of his clan.

"Let us hope," Lord Rutherford replied coldly, "that your hospitality is more substantial than your reputation, *young* laird."

Ewan clenched his jaw, struggling to maintain his composure in the face of such blatant disrespect. He knew that he could not afford to let his emotions get the better of him, for the sake of his clan and the fragile peace they sought with the English lord. But as he looked around the great hall at the faces of his people, their eyes filled with hope and apprehension, Ewan could not help but wonder if he had what it took to lead them through the tumultuous days ahead.

And then his eyes fell on Maeve, and everything changed.

She stood in the shadows of the great hall, half-hidden behind a pillar, her brilliant green eyes narrowed slightly as though in thought. She gazed at Lord Rutherford, her teeth worrying her lower lip, and yet there was no sign of unease upon her face. Instead, Ewan saw something powerful and strong and determined, and as the lights of the candles danced upon her auburn tresses, once more making her glowing, Ewan could hardly believe that she was of this earth.

A woman of flesh and blood.

And then Maeve looked up and their eyes met. They seemed to drill into his own as though they were linked somehow, by some unseen bond. *Believe in yerself, Ewan. Believe in yerself as I do.*

Ewan heard her voice echoing through his mind, and it felt as though she had whispered in his ear, as though she stood right beside him and not across the hall. It was a strange sensation, and yet it lifted the weight off his chest and allowed him to draw back his shoulders with an easy smile upon his lips. "Please, join us for supper," Ewan said to Lord Rutherford with as much warmth as he could muster as the cloak of worry that had lain draped upon his shoulders fell to the floor, almost forgotten. He gestured toward the long table that had been set up in the great hall, laden with fresh food.

"Very well," Lord Rutherford agreed with a curt nod, his footsteps echoing through the hall as he followed Ewan to the table. As they took their seats, Ewan suddenly felt Maeve's reassuring presence beside him, and as he turned, she stood right there, looking up at him, her green eyes filled with quiet determination. Her hand briefly settled upon his arm, her touch an immeasurable comfort to his soul, and he pulled out her chair for her before seating himself between Maeve and Lord Rutherford.

Allowing his gaze to sweep over the great hall, Ewan caught Drystan's eye from a nearby table and was momentarily taken aback by the intensity of the man's glare. He recalled their heated confrontation earlier that day when Drystan had voiced his doubts about Ewan's ability to stand up to the likes of Rutherford. The memory of Drystan's words stung, but Ewan knew he could not let those doubts consume him. He had a responsibility to his people, and he would not allow himself to be intimidated by the English lord sitting beside him —neither by one of his own men.

"May I offer ye some wine, Lord Rutherford?" Ewan asked, reaching for the pitcher on the table and doing his best to maintain a calm and confident demeanor.

"Thank you, Laird MacDrummond," Lord Rutherford replied, extending his goblet to be filled. "I must say, I've heard quite a lot about your father since embarking upon this journey. A formidable man, from what I remember."

Ewan's heart clenched at the mention of his late father, but he forced a smile as he nodded. "Aye, he was. I hope to honor his legacy in my own way."

"Indeed," Lord Rutherford murmured, swirling the wine in his goblet before taking a sip. "Well then, let us pray—for your sake—that your way proves to be more effective than your father's, hm?"

Ewan clenched his jaw, momentarily taken aback by the other man's unveiled insult. Then, though, he felt a soft weight upon his arm, a touch so gentle and yet so powerful that it gave him pause before the anger brewing inside of him could spill forth.

Maeve's gaze was warm and soothing as Ewan turned his eyes to her, and the smile that curled up his lips at seeing her thus felt utterly genuine.

Nay, he would not give Lord Rutherford the satisfaction of getting under his skin. He would not!

And so, instead of doing something unwise, Ewan took a deep breath and let his gaze wander across the table as the servants began to serve the meal. "Please, enjoy the food my people have prepared," he said politely, trying to keep the conversation on neutral ground. "I trust ye'll find it quite to yer liking."

As the evening wore on, Ewan did his best to engage Lord Rutherford in polite conversation, all the while feeling the weight of Drystan's doubt and the lingering echo of his father's legacy bearing down on him. But whenever he felt overwhelmed, he need only glance at Maeve beside him, her unwavering strength and quiet support helping to steady him through the storm.

The fire crackled in the enormous hearth, casting flickering shadows across the great hall that seemed to dance in time with Ewan's pounding heart. Where tense silence had reigned before, his people were now actively engaged in conversation, laughter even ringing out here and there.

Though still on edge—how could it be any different considering the magnitude of Lord Rutherford's visit?—Ewan felt himself relax as well, knowing Maeve was by his side. Her presence was like a warm fire in the deep of winter, chasing away the chill that threatened to engulf him. He could not help but smile at her, and as his gaze wandered across the hall and over the faces of his people, Ewan realized that not all were filled with doubt. Certainly, there were those like Drystan who believed he could never fill his father's shoes. Yet he also saw others, nodding to him in encouragement and approval.

"MacDrummond," Rutherford began, pausing to tear a piece of bread from the loaf before him. "I think it's high time we discuss the terms of the settlement."

"Tomorrow, my lord," Ewan replied, striving to keep his voice steady. If there was one thing his father had taught him, it was not to allow another to dictate his actions. "The early hours of the day are better suited for matters of business." He locked eyes with Rutherford, silently daring the old English fox to argue.

Rutherford's brow furrowed, and the corners of his mouth turned downward in clear displeasure. Yet he held his tongue, returning his focus to the meal before him.

Feeling the weight of the man's disapproval, Ewan felt his muscles tense as his doubts return like a swarm of bees. Instinctively, he glanced at Maeve, seated on his other side, and the moment her green eyes met his, warm and unwavering, like a beacon of hope amidst the stormy sea of his thoughts, the pressure in his chest eased ever so slightly.

Aye, she was like a miracle to Ewan, risen from the ground like a wood sprite, the fire in her eyes one he had never seen before and her whispers like the echo of his own heart.

Remain calm, Ewan. He will try to bait ye. Dunna give in! Ewan swallowed hard as Maeve's voice once more echoed through his mind, so clear as if she had spoken out loud.

"Tell me, Lord Rutherford," Ewan said, turning his attention back to the imposing man beside him, "have ye ever been to the Scottish Highlands in autumn? The colors are truly a sight to behold."

"Indeed," Rutherford replied, his tone guarded but not entirely dismissive. "The beauty of the landscape is one of the few things I find agreeable about these lands."

"Ah, then perhaps ye might enjoy a ride through our hills tomorrow after we've settled matters?" Ewan suggested, doing his best to maintain an air of camaraderie. "I could have some horses saddled for us."

"Perhaps," Rutherford conceded, his expression softening just a touch. "We shall see."

They continued their conversation, with Ewan making every effort to steer the discussion toward less contentious topics. The more he spoke with Rutherford, the more he came to understand that there was more to the old Englishman than a cold heart.

Perhaps not even that. If only he knew what lay underneath?

Ewan's thoughts churned, considering every angle, every possibility, and all the while, Maeve remained a steadfast presence at his side, her quiet support giving him the strength to weather the storm of uncertainty that had threatened to consume him before.

Chapter Thirteen

A STORYTELLER OF OLD

The great hall of Castle MacDrummond was alive with the murmur of conversation and the clatter of cutlery against plates. Torches flickered on the walls, casting an amber glow over the long tables filled with steaming dishes of venison, roasted vegetables, and freshly baked bread. Maeve sat between Ewan and his aunt Innes, the tension as palpable as the heat from the hearth as all their thoughts strayed to the English lord in their midst. Curious glances were cast in his direction from all sides, some veiled and others obvious. Aunt Innes had a constant scowl upon her face, her lips pressed into a tight line and her eyes narrowed as she scrutinized Lord Rutherford.

The stakes were high, and everyone in the room seemed to hold their breath, waiting for either diplomacy or disaster to unfold before them.

Nevertheless, Maeve felt proud of Ewan as she observed him conversing politely with Lord Rutherford. His calm demeanor and steady voice were a testament to his resolve, a young laird striving to protect his people and uphold his family's legacy. She knew that he had doubted himself—that he still did—but now she felt justified in her belief in him. All he needed was a little help, and perhaps she could provide it.

Her gaze shifted to Lord Rutherford, studying the lines of his face and the cold, calculating glint in his eyes. What sort of man was he, truly? What secrets hid behind that mask of authority and arrogance? Would she be able to uncover anything that could be of use to Ewan in his negotiations?

Maeve could not deny that there was hesitation within her. After denying her ability for so long, it felt strange to even consider tapping into them now. Yet the thoughts she had gleaned earlier this day from Ewan as well as others allowed her to better judge her capabilities. If she stayed focused, the hum of voices—of thoughts—would not overwhelm her, and perhaps she could glean something of vital importance.

Maeve watched as Lord Rutherford took a sip of his wine, his lips curling in distaste as he set the goblet down with a resounding thud. His eyes scanned the great hall, lingering on the banners and tapestries that adorned the walls, before settling on the fur-clad clansmen sharing stories and laughter at the far end of the room. It was clear that he held little regard for their customs, judging by the sneer that danced across his face.

"Highland fare is certainly... unique," he drawled, pushing aside his plate with a stern expression. "I imagine it takes some getting used to."

"Indeed, my lord," Ewan replied diplomatically, his voice steady even though Maeve could sense the annoyance flickering beneath his calm exterior. "Our people take pride in their traditions and have adapted well to the rugged landscape and harsh climate."

"Admirable," Lord Rutherford said dismissively, picking at his food with disinterest. "But I daresay they would benefit from a touch of refinement."

Maeve bristled at the Englishman's condescending tone, and her admiration for Ewan grew that he managed to remain calm under these challenging circumstances. Aye, he was a good and strong man, and she did not doubt that he would grow into this new position so unexpectedly thrust at him.

Resolved to aid Ewan any way she could, Maeve closed her eyes for a brief moment and allowed herself to become attuned to the murmurings of Lord Rutherford's mind.

At first, the hum swelled like a wave crashing toward shore, and Maeve pressed her lips together tightly to keep a gasp from slipping out and perhaps drawing Ewan's attention. She breathed in deeply and then out, and soon snippets of Lord Rutherford's disdain for the Highlands and their customs echoed through her head. Indeed, he believed that these people were uncouth savages who needed to be tamed by the civilizing hand of England. Yet among the contempt and arrogance, Maeve sensed an echo of something else: a deep-rooted pain that seemed to gnaw at his very soul.

Sudden silence fell over the great hall as Ewan rose from his seat, and Maeve felt her concentration slip and Lord Rutherford's thoughts withdraw. "In honor of our esteemed guest," Ewan announced, a warm smile upon his face as he looked at his people, "I have arranged for a special treat tonight. We have with us a renowned storyteller, who shall regale us with tales of the Old Ones."

The atmosphere in the room shifted as anticipation and curiosity swept through the gathered clan members, their whispered conversations ceasing as they turned their attention toward the center of the room. Maeve could feel her own excitement building, her heart racing at the prospect of the ancient stories that would soon be shared. She remembered vague tales from her childhood, shared around a warm fire, yet long years had passed since she had last heard a story.

At this announcement, Lord Rutherford's expression darkened, his lips pressing into a thin line as he regarded the unfolding scene with palpable disdain. "How... quaint," he muttered under his breath, clearly unimpressed by Ewan's gesture. Maeve clenched her fists beneath the table, struggling to keep her composure in the face of such blatant disrespect, and focused her attention on the bearded, gray-haired man, taking his place before the gathering.

A hush fell over the room, and with a voice like the wind rustling through autumn leaves, the old man began to weave a tale that captivated both young and old. It was a story of the Old Ones—ancient beings said to have once walked the earth alongside mortals, their magic flowing through the land like lifeblood.

"Long ago," the storyteller began, "the Old Ones shaped the very mountains and valleys we now call home. They were beings of immense power but with hearts full of wisdom and love. They gifted their knowledge to those they deemed worthy, bestowing upon them abilities beyond imagination, hoping to aid people in their quest for unity and peace."

Maeve felt her pulse quicken as the story unfolded, the images painted by the storyteller's words stirring something deep within her soul. She thought of her own ability, so long a source of fear and isolation, and suddenly wondered if the Old Ones had once bestowed their gifts upon her ancestors. Could her own power be a legacy of these ancient beings? And if so, what did it mean for her future?

Maeve's eyes flicked to Ewan, who sat enraptured by the story. She could see the pride in his eyes as the storyteller spoke of the great deeds of their ancestors, and she knew that his heart longed to follow in their footsteps—to be a laird worthy of his clan's history.

When the story reached its end, the room was silent for a moment, the powerful words still lingering in the air like echoes of a forgotten past. Then, with quiet murmurs of appreciation, the clan members began to break off into small groups, discussing the tale and speculating on its meaning.

As Maeve reflected on the story, she felt something stir within her—a newfound sense of purpose and acceptance. For the first time in her life, she began to view her ability not as a curse but as a gift, a legacy that connected her to a lineage of power and magic. If she could harness this power and use it to help Ewan, perhaps they could forge a new future for his clan—one filled with hope and unity.

"Truly a captivating tale," Ewan declared, addressing the gathered clan members. "It reminds us all of the strength and power that lies within each of us."

Lord Rutherford scoffed, clearly unimpressed by the ancient legend. "Superstitious nonsense," he muttered under his breath, swirling the last of his wine in his goblet. "These Highlanders and their primitive tales... Come now, we have more important matters to discuss."

Maeve watched as Ewan's jaw tightened, but he remained

composed, turning to Lord Rutherford with a polite smile. "Of course, my lord. We shall continue our negotiations in the morning. For now, allow me to show ye to the chamber I had prepared for ye."

As Ewan led Lord Rutherford away, he glanced over his shoulder and their eyes met. Maeve smiled at him, and he nodded, assuring her that he would return shortly.

Slowly, the clan members dispersed, and Maeve rose from her seat and ventured over to the large hearth, her gaze drawn to the dancing flames, her thoughts racing. She felt deeply grateful for the storyteller's tale, for its words resonated deep within her soul, shedding new light on her once-feared ability. It was an affirmation that what she possessed was not a curse but rather a powerful tool given to her for a greater purpose. And with this revelation came a growing sense of certainty that she was no longer alone in the world, that—unexpected as it was—she had found a place for herself, her duty now to ensure the well-being of those she cared for.

"Did ye enjoy the story, lass?" Aunt Innes asked, appearing beside Maeve. A kind smile rested on the old woman's face, and she looked rather fatigued.

"More than I can say," Maeve replied softly, feeling a warmth in her chest as she looked at Ewan's aunt. "I believe... it has helped me understand myself better." Though aware of a need for caution, Maeve felt increasingly uncomfortable speaking half-truths at every turn. "It made me think about the part I am to play... in helping Ewan."

For a moment, Aunt Innes regarded her shrewdly, and Maeve all but held her breath. Then the old woman nodded. "Ah, the Old Ones have a way of guiding us when we need it most," she agreed, her eyes twinkling with wisdom. "Now, go on, get some rest. Tomorrow will be a long day."

Maeve nodded, grateful for Aunt Innes's kind words despite their rocky beginning. Who knew, perhaps one day...?

As she turned to leave, Ewan reappeared in the hall, and the way his eyes lit up when he beheld her, brought tears to Maeve's eyes. *He cares for me, does he not?* She sighed, blinking them away. *And I care for him. Heaven help me, but I do.*

“May I escort ye to yer chamber,” Ewan asked, his eyes aglow, as he offered her his arm. “’Tis been a long night.”

Maeve nodded, accepting his offer and welcoming his presence. At his touch, his warmth reached out to her, and she almost leaned into him. “Aye, ’tis true,” she told him as they left the great hall, and he guided her through the dimly lit corridors toward her chamber. “A beautiful one, though.” She smiled up at him. “I loved the storyteller. His words were wonderful.”

Ewan nodded on a deep exhale, his thoughts clearly elsewhere. “The evening went better than I anticipated,” he admitted, a hint of relief in his voice. “Ye were a great help, Maeve. Thank ye for standing by me.”

“Of course, Ewan” she replied softly, feeling a swell of pride at his words. She could not recall the last time someone—anyone—had had need of her. “I’ll always support ye.”

“Ye ken,” Ewan continued thoughtfully, “there were moments when I felt as though I…” He paused, almost shaking his head as though to chase away a most ludicrous thought.

“As though?” Maeve pressed, wishing for him to share his thoughts, unwilling to intrude yet again. Aye, once had been enough, and the thought still plagued her.

Ewan chuckled sheepishly. “As though I could hear yer voice in my ear, whispering, urging me to believe in myself. ’Twas… strange, but strangely comforting.” Again, he chuckled, meeting her eyes, his own aglow with relief and joy.

Maeve swallowed hard. “Aye, it does sound strange,” she murmured as her mind raced. Could her thoughts have truly reached Ewan’s mind, or was it simply a coincidence? She hesitated before saying more, suddenly terrified yet again to reveal her secret. “Perhaps we’re more connected than we realized.”

“Perhaps,” Ewan agreed, his gaze lingering upon hers as they stopped outside her chamber door. “Perhaps I was meant to find ye that day in the woods. Perhaps ye called to me.”

A shiver danced down Maeve’s spine, and her breath was suddenly far from steady. “Do ye believe so?”

Ewan nodded, his eyes still fixed upon hers as he shifted closer, and

Maeve felt his touch upon her waist. "Would ye mind...?" he began then chuckled, once more a sheepish expression appeared upon his face. "I have to admit ye've been quite the distraction."

"Me?" Maeve exclaimed, surprised by this sudden change in direction. In fact, a moment ago, she had been certain Ewan had been on the brink of stealing a kiss—one she would have been most willing to grant.

"Ye were on my mind all night," Ewan murmured, tugging her a little closer. "I could sense ye right there by my side, yer warmth," he leaned in and brushed a tender kiss onto her right temple, "yer soft whispers," his lips traced her left temple until she could feel his breath upon her own, "yer trust in me." Before Maeve could even think of a response, Ewan's mouth captured hers in a passionate kiss, revealing all he felt and hoped for.

Much too soon, he pulled back, though, a warm smile upon his lips as he bent to kiss her hand in a most gallant gesture. "Well, then, goodnight, Maeve. Sleep well."

"Goodnight, Ewan." Maeve's voice sounded breathless to her own ears, and she had to lean against her door for balance as she watched him disappear down the hallway, her thoughts racing.

As was her heart.

Yet there was no time to dwell upon private desires; and so, with a cautious glance up and down the corridor, Maeve left behind the safety of her chamber and carefully picked her way through the darkened castle, determined to learn what secrets lay hidden within the English lord's heart.

Her footsteps were light as she made her way toward Lord Rutherford's chamber, her senses heightened by the stillness of her surroundings. As she approached, she saw a servant exit his room, leaving the door slightly ajar. Maeve pressed herself against the cold stone wall, out of sight, her heart pounding in her chest.

"Very well, then," Lord Rutherford's voice drifted out from within, the disdain in his tone unmistakable. "I shall retire for the night. Remember, I expect my breakfast to be prompt and hot."

"Of course, milord," came the muffled reply as the servant hurried away.

Holding her breath, Maeve edged closer to the door, straining to hear any further conversation. Then she closed her eyes and took a deep breath, steeling herself for the intimate act of entering another's thoughts. She recalled the sensation of being inside Ewan's mind earlier that evening—the warm familiarity of his thoughts. The memory of his gratitude washed over her, giving her the courage to proceed.

Focusing on Lord Rutherford's presence within the chamber, she felt the barrier between their minds begin to weaken. Slowly, she let her own thoughts seep through the cracks, seeking out any useful information that might help Ewan in his quest to protect his clan.

An image of a woman appeared in Maeve's mind, beautiful and regal, with sorrowful eyes that seemed to pierce through her very soul. A name echoed in her head, whispered with such longing and heartache that it nearly took her breath away: *Eleanor*.

Chapter Fourteen
A MARVELOUS TIME

Ewan awoke with a start, his heart pounding in his chest. The morning sun, tinged orange and red, filtered through the heavy curtains, casting long shadows across the stone floor. He rubbed his eyes, attempting to dispel the lingering remnants of sleep. Today was the day of the negotiation with Lord Rutherford, and Ewan's stomach twisted with anxiety. His heart, though, longed only for Maeve.

Indeed, he had only bade her good night a few precious hours ago, and yet it already felt as though too much time had passed since he had last laid eyes on her. She was like the sun to him, like the air he breathed, and even a moment of absence cast him into darkness. More than anything, he wanted to rush to her side, embrace her once again, feel her close.

Ewan heaved a heavy, rather wistful sigh, knowing it was not possible just yet. There were more pressing matters to attend to, and he could not shirk his responsibilities.

Sitting up, he ran a hand through his disheveled black hair as his father's dying words once more echoed in his mind: *protect the clan at all costs*. The memory sent a shiver down Ewan's spine, as if the ghost of his father were watching over him, urging him not to fail.

Gathering himself, Ewan dressed quickly and left his chamber, then he proceeded toward Maeve's. Unfortunately, they only had a few moments alone together—not nearly enough—before descending the staircase into the great hall.

The hearth roared with a crackling fire, warding off the early morning chill. Servants scurried about, setting the table with plates of steaming porridge, fresh bread, and smoked fish. The scent of roasted meat and spices filled the air, tantalizing his senses but doing nothing to calm his nerves.

Only the warmth of Maeve's hand upon his arm soothed the tension that lingered, and he smiled at her, guiding her to her seat, before taking his own.

Clearly an early riser, Lord Rutherford already occupied the same seat he had the night before, his presence a dark cloud that loomed over the vaulted chamber. With a furrowed brow and stormy countenance, the powerful English lord looked every bit the formidable opponent he was known to be. Ewan's fingers twitched involuntarily, his apprehension palpable.

"Good morning, Lord Rutherford," Ewan said, forcing a tight-lipped smile. "I hope ye slept well."

"Indeed, Laird MacDrummond," Lord Rutherford replied curtly, his voice cold and unwelcoming. "Yer hospitality is most appreciated."

The tension in the great hall was nearly suffocating, as the other occupants engaged in polite but meaningless conversation. Ewan could feel the weight of their stares, as if they, too, were waiting for some spark to ignite the powder keg of emotions that lay beneath the surface.

As the breakfast progressed, the air in the room grew heavier with unspoken words and veiled intentions, each man holding his cards close to his chest. But Ewan's resolve hardened, knowing that his clan's future rested on his ability to navigate the treacherous waters ahead. Today, he would need all the strength and wisdom his father had bestowed upon him and be the man Maeve saw in him.

For his clan.

For her.

For himself.

With a final sip of his ale, Ewan rose from his seat, steeling himself for the challenge that awaited him in the meeting chamber. The ghosts of the past hovered just out of sight, but he would not be deterred. For the sake of his people and the memory of his father, he would find a way to forge an alliance with the enigmatic Lord Rutherford—or die trying.

Striding down the dimly lit corridor, Ewan felt his heart pounding in his chest like a drum as the heavy oak door of the meeting chamber loomed ahead, taunting him with the unknown.

"Wait," a soft voice called out to him, halting Ewan in his tracks. Maeve appeared from the shadows, her auburn hair cascading over her shoulders and her emerald eyes shimmering as though she carried a light within. "There's something ye needa ken, Ewan."

Ewan's heart skipped a beat as he met her gaze, and yet again he unable to shake the feeling that there was more to Maeve than met the eye. She had an uncanny ability for knowing things she should not, and while it unnerved him, it also intrigued him. "What is it?" he asked, his voice barely above a whisper.

"Lord Rutherford..." Maeve hesitated, worrying her lower lip, as though all courage had suddenly left her. There was even a trace of fear in her eyes; it vanished quickly, though, and she forged ahead. "He... He has suffered a recent loss, one that has struck him deeply."

Ewan frowned, inching closer, his right hand coming to rest upon her waist as though it belonged there. Perhaps it did. "How do ye ken this?"

Maeve pressed her lips into a tight line before she slowly shook her head. "I'm sorry. I canna tell ye that." Her hands reached up and cupped his face, her skin soft and warm against his own. "Please, Ewan, trust me. Rutherford... He... He isna as cold as he might seem. There is pain in his past. I'm certain that... that he has lost someone most dear to him." A sad smile teased her lips as she held his gaze. "Not unlike ye lost yer father."

Ewan raised an eyebrow. "How does this help me?" he questioned, the pressure of the upcoming negotiation weighing heavily on his mind.

Maeve sighed, something deeply gentle in her gaze. "Everyone has their vulnerabilities, Ewan. Even the coldest hearts can be warmed by understanding and compassion," she whispered, her eyes searching his, pleading for him to grasp the significance of her words. "If ye can find common ground with Lord Rutherford, a shared connection, then ye stand a better chance at succeeding in these negotiations."

Ewan paused, considering Maeve's advice, surprised it had not occurred to him. He had spent so much time preparing for a battle of wits that he had not considered the power of empathy and understanding. Yet how could he truly find a bond with a man as cold and calculating as Lord Rutherford?

Remembering the man's hard gaze, doubt clawed at his heart. Still, Maeve's eyes shone with trust and faith, and despite their short acquaintance, Ewan knew that she possessed a keen insight into the hearts of others. Had she not done the same for him?

"Thank ye, Maeve," Ewan said, his voice filled with gratitude. "I will heed yer words... even though I admit I dunna quite ken how to go about it." He offered her a tentative smile.

"Ye'll find a way," Maeve assured him before she pushed herself up and onto her toes, pressing a gentle kiss to his lips. "Just remember that ye're not alone in yer struggles—we all carry our own burdens and heartaches." Pain swung in her voice, and her eyes reflected a depth of experience far beyond her years. *One day, I will ken what happened*, Ewan vowed silently, *and I will do what I can to heal yer heart.*

With a nod, Ewan turned and continued toward the meeting chamber door, his resolve strengthened by Maeve's counsel. If there was a chance to find common ground with Lord Rutherford, then he would seize it.

Inhaling a deep breath, Ewan entered the meeting chamber, a room filled with shadows and echoes of past negotiations. Heavy tapestries adorned the walls, depicting clan battles and ancient legends. The air hung thick with tension, laden with the scent of burning candles and polished wood. At the far end of the long oak table, Lord Rutherford sat rigidly, his face an unreadable mask, men of his entourage by his side. Cromartie and two other advisors, who had already served Ewan's father, waited at the table's other end.

Two oppositions.

Was there truly a way to find common ground? He could not help but have doubts.

"Lord Rutherford," Ewan greeted, the words coming out sharper than intended. His heart thudded in his chest, as he remembered Maeve's advice to find a bond with the English lord.

"MacDrummond," Rutherford replied curtly, his piercing blue eyes narrowing slightly. "Let us not waste time. I trust you have considered my demands?"

Ewan took his seat at the head of the table, feeling the weight of generations upon him. He glanced around at all those assembled here, their expressions ranging from hope to apprehension, and he realized in that moment that what was needed was... privacy.

Aye, one could not bear one's heart under the watchful gaze of others, and thus Ewan once more rose to his feet. "Indeed, I have," he began, his voice surprisingly steady. "Before we proceed, though, I must ask ye," he met Lord Rutherford's gaze, "to grant me a moment of yer time." His brows rose before he swept his gaze over the assembled men. "Alone."

The room fell into a hushed silence, all eyes shifting to Lord Rutherford. His brow furrowed, but there was a flicker of surprise in his eyes.

Ewan pressed on, allowing Lord Rutherford a glimpse at his own vulnerability. "I have something to say that is meant for yer ears alone." Then he nodded to Cromartie, and, although reluctantly, his trusted advisor ushered the other two clansmen out of the chamber.

"Very well," Lord Rutherford agreed, dismissing his entourage with a wave of his hand. One by one, they all filed out of the chamber until the heavy oak door fell closed behind them. "What is it you have to say?"

Ewan gestured toward the two cushioned armchairs in front of the hearth. "Let us sit here instead of far apart at this long table. Perhaps it'll be easier to find common ground this way."

Again, Ewan thought to see a flicker of surprise in Rutherford's gaze before the old lord rose to his feet and took the proffered chair. "I admit you have me intrigued."

Seating himself, Ewan exhaled a slow breath, considering how to begin. "Ye knew my father," he stated simply, meeting Lord Rutherford's gaze. "Ye ken he was a strong man, cautious and always acting with forethought. Every day, he rose to do the best for our clan, and our people trusted in him." He heaved a heavy sigh, holding the other man's gaze, wondering how Lord Rutherford would react to his next words. "Yet most of all, I miss the father he was to me."

Rutherford barely moved, only the slight rise and fall of his chest setting him apart from the stillness resting upon the rest of the chamber.

Praying that he had the other man's ear, Ewan allowed his gaze to drift away, remembering the moment he had known his father to be gone. "I never expected to lose him," he murmured. "Not so soon. I thought... there'd be more time, more..." He shrugged. "Sometimes, I still feel him nearby, as though I only need turn a corner and... he's there." A heavy lump formed in his throat as he gazed across the chamber toward the end of the long table where his father had often sat. "There are moments when the world feels as it always did, moments when his loss doesna even feel real." He raked a hand through his hair, feeling tears linger in the corners of his eyes. "And then there are others when I feel his loss so acutely that... I'm certain I canna bear it another moment." He lifted his gaze and met Rutherford's eyes. "My clan lost their laird, but I lost my father and I dunna yet feel ready to go on without him." Ewan's pulse thundered in his veins, fear warring with faith, whispering that he had just shown an irredeemable weakness to his enemy.

And the sly old fox would surely pounce on it!

Only he did not.

Instead, Rutherford studied Ewan for a moment, something unspoken passing between them. Aye, the man's surprise was palpable as his dark eyes widened ever so slightly. His cold, calculating demeanor that had enveloped him throughout their conversations before began to waver, as if Ewan's vulnerability had touched something deep within him. Then, as if a dam had broken, he exhaled heavily, his shoulders slumping in defeat. "How did you know?" he asked simply.

Ewan exhaled deeply. "A... friend suggested that ye... were in pain, and I thought that was something we had in common."

Lord Rutherford nodded, and his cold, hard exterior melted away, making him look old and frail and heart-broken. "My granddaughter," he whispered, his voice choked and his jaw tight as he fought for composure. "Eleanor died in childbirth only a few months past. She was the light of my life, and her death has left a void that can never be filled."

Ewan's heart clenched at the raw pain in the old man's voice, understanding all too well the ache of loss. "Lord Rutherford, I am truly sorry for yer loss," Ewan murmured, his voice heavy with genuine sympathy.

Aye, now he could see the man Maeve had glimpsed, the man behind the facade—a grieving grandfather, struggling with the weight of his own loss, and despite their shared loss, the tension in the room seemed to lessen, replaced by a fragile thread of commonality. They were two men bound by their heartache, each grasping for a lifeline amidst the darkness.

"Parents ought not survive their children," Lord Rutherford murmured, his gaze drifting to the dancing flames in the heart. "Let alone their grandchildren."

"Aye, 'tis heartbreaking. What... What of her bairn?" Ewan asked cautiously. "Her child?"

The ghost of a smile flitted across Rutherford's face. "A daughter," he murmured, and he lifted a hand to brush a lone tear from the corner of his eye. "She has her mother's dark curls, and Eleanor's husband gave her her mother's name."

"That is good," Ewan replied, unable to imagine such a loss. Yet what if he were to lose Maeve? The thought caused him physical pain, and he realized what he had not dared before: he loved her with all his heart and soul. "Take comfort in wee Eleanor then, for she'll forever remind ye of her mother, keeping her with ye for as long as ye shall live."

Lord Rutherford nodded slowly, a newfound respect gleaming in his gaze as the two men regarded one another with new eyes. Aye, the silence that settled between them was a fragile thing, weighted with the memory of their losses. Ewan studied Lord Rutherford's face, searching for any hint of deceit, but found only sincerity in the older man's eyes.

"Tell me, MacDrummond," Lord Rutherford finally broke the silence, his voice softer than before, "What is it you wish to propose? I can see there's something on your mind."

Ewan hesitated for a moment, feeling the weight of his responsibility bearing down on him. He knew that the path forward would require compromise from both sides, yet for the first time since his father's passing, Ewan looked into the future with a hopeful heart.

Chapter Fifteen

TWO VULNERABLE MEN

The cool, damp air clung to Maeve's skin as she paced nervously outside the meeting chamber. Her auburn hair whipped around her face, the tendrils sticking to her cheeks and her eyes no doubt filled with the worry that weighed heavily upon her chest. She glanced over her shoulder, noting that the advisors had left some time ago, leaving only Ewan and Lord Rutherford within the chamber's heavy wooden doors. If only she knew what was happening inside!

Maeve bit her lip, her heart pounding in her chest as the temptation to use her abilities suddenly roared to life, gnawing at her resolve. After spending years suppressing it, ignoring it, pretending it was not there, she was surprised to see how quickly she had grown used to its presence within the span of a mere day. Did that perhaps mean it was a part of her? That her abilities were a gift like so many others. Aye, now that it was free, it no longer plagued her, at least not the way it had before.

Still, despite her excitement, Maeve reminded herself that it was wrong to invade another's privacy without their permission. Only the most dire of circumstances would justify such a breach; however, the thought of Ewan, the man who had shown her kindness and understanding when she needed it most, being alone with the cold and calculating Lord Rutherford filled her with dread.

"Come on, Maeve," she whispered to herself, "ye've made it this far. Ye can do this." She took a deep breath, trying to steady her nerves and focus on the importance of respecting Ewan's trust, as well as Lord Rutherford's. Unfortunately, the stone walls of the castle still seemed to close in on Maeve, the weight of her isolation pressing down on her like a heavy shroud. If only she had someone to confide in! Someone to hold her hand and wait out here with her!

Aye, isolation was no way to live, and yet... would she ever feel comfortable sharing all she was with those in her life?

As Maeve continued to pace, her thoughts circled back to the task at hand. This negotiation could change everything for Ewan, for his clan, and... perhaps even for herself? If only she could be certain of its outcome without betraying the confidence of those within the chamber.

"Patience," Maeve reminded herself, clenching her fists at her sides. "Ye must have faith in Ewan. He has faced challenges before, and he will rise to meet them again."

With each step, Maeve felt the pull of her abilities growing stronger, the whispers from behind the door tempting her like a siren's song. It took all her willpower to resist the urge to listen in on the conversation, to know what was happening within those walls. "Trust," she repeated under her breath. "'Tis a test of yer faith in others, and in yerself." *Perhaps by the Old Ones?*

As Maeve continued to pace, the tension in the air grew thick, anticipation coiling like a serpent around her heart. But she held on to her resolve, knowing that whatever the outcome, she needed to be steadfast.

After a small eternity, the door to the chamber finally creaked open, and Maeve's breath hitched in her throat. Her heart pounded as she watched Ewan and Lord Rutherford emerge from the room, their expressions unreadable. Yet, as they stepped into the light of the torchlit hallway, she noticed a subtle change in their postures—shoulders relaxed, heads held high, even the faint trace of a smile upon their faces. A glimmer of newfound respect seemed to pass between them, perhaps a mutual understanding forged through shared pain?

"Trust," Maeve reminded herself once more, allowing the tension within her to dissipate as she took in the sight before her. "Ewan!" His name fell from her lips without thought, and Maeve instantly clamped a hand over her mouth as though the movement could retrieve it, her cheeks flushing red with embarrassment.

Of course, both men turned to look in her direction, and Maeve felt not only Ewan's gaze touch her face but also Rutherford's. The old lord's gaze narrowed slightly before his gaze shifted to Ewan. "The friend you spoke of?"

Maeve froze, staring as Ewan nodded, a smile upon his face. "Aye." Then his eyes met hers, and Maeve felt her heart pause in her chest, soft shivers dancing across her skin.

Rutherford inhaled a long breath and inclined his head to Maeve in a gesture of respect that caught her completely off guard. In the next instant, though, the old lord was already striding down the corridor, calling for his advisors.

With a wide smile upon his face, Ewan rushed toward her, his hands grasping hers as words flew from his lips, his grey eyes aglow with relief and joy. "Ye were right, Maeve," he said softly, the weight of the world seemingly lifted from his shoulders. "In sharing our grief, we've found common ground."

Maeve's heart swelled with pride and affection for the man before her, and her hands tightened upon his. "Truly?"

He nodded and for a moment closed his eyes, his face lined with recent grief. Aye, Maeve could see that he had heeded her advice, that he had shared his grief with Rutherford. She could also see that it had been far from easy for him, and she felt proud of him.

Of herself as well.

A little.

After all, had she not used her abilities to bring about a difference here? Had she not used them to change what could have ended in disaster? Aye, together, they had surmounted an obstacle that had once seemed insurmountable, and it felt good.

"Ye did it, Ewan," Maeve whispered, squeezing his hands for reassurance. "We did it, together."

As their fingers intertwined, the connection between them felt stronger than ever; an unbreakable bond forged through trust and...

Maeve paused, and she felt cold, icy tendrils snaking across her skin. Aye, Ewan trusted her, but was he right to do so? Even though she had not violated his thoughts today, she had the day before. And she might again at any moment in time... and he had no notion of even the possibility of that happening. Was that trust?

Tell him, a voice deep inside whispered, and Maeve lifted her head and parted her lips, the words upon the tip of her tongue.

In that moment, though, Ewan stepped forward and the distance between them vanished as he enveloped her in a warm embrace, his strong arms wrapping around her slender frame protectively.

Despite the tears that pricked her eyes, Maeve leaned into his chest, unable to help herself. She closed her eyes, savoring the closeness they shared, feeling his heartbeat against her own.

"Thank ye, Maeve," Ewan murmured into her hair, his breath tickling her ear. "I dinna ken if I could have done it without ye."

Maeve felt a surge of affection for the man who held her so tenderly. It was moments like these that reminded her of why she had chosen to trust him despite the fear that had once held her captive. Aye, she had been right to trust him, but could the same be said for him? If she told him, would he be furious with her for betraying him?

"Ye are stronger than ye ken," Maeve replied softly, her words muffled by the fabric of his shirt. "All ye needed was a wee bit o' encouragement."

As Ewan pulled back, his face held a mixture of relief and pride, and Maeve quickly blinked her eyes to chase away the tears that lingered nearby. "Aye, perhaps," he agreed, a small smile playing on his lips. "Yet 'twas more than just encouragement. Ye helped me see that sharing our grief could bring us together. When I opened up to Rutherford about losing my father, he shared his own loss—the death of his granddaughter."

Maeve's heart clenched painfully, compassion sweeping through her as she understood the depth of Lord Rutherford's loss. Indeed, it seemed that even the coldest of hearts could be thawed by empathy and understanding.

"By finding common ground in our sorrow, we were able to see each other not as enemies, but as men who've suffered greatly," Ewan continued, his voice filled with newfound wisdom. "And from there, we found more common ground." He chuckled, a touch of disbelief to it. "As it is, Lord Rutherford is a man just as concerned for the well-being of his people as I am for mine." He sighed, his hands holding Maeve's tightly within his own. "A terrible flood destroyed most of their crops, and he came here looking for a way to feed his people." He swallowed. "Just as my father went to Rutherford after the war seeking aid."

Maeve nodded. "Though it might seem so, we are not all that different from one another, are we?" *Perhaps I am, though!*

"Yer advice made all the difference, Maeve. Ye've helped me see that there is strength in vulnerability, and that by sharing our deepest sorrows, we can bridge even the widest divides." Ewan's grey eyes held a warmth and gratitude that made Maeve's heart swell with pride and ache with regret.

Chapter Sixteen

THE RIGHTFUL LAIRD

The great hall of Castle MacDrummond brimmed with tension, the flickering torchlight casting long shadows on the stone walls. Ewan and Lord Rutherford stood shoulder to shoulder at the head of the room, facing a sea of expectant faces. The gathered MacDrummond clan members and Rutherford's entourage waited in hushed anticipation for what was to come.

Ewan felt the weight of responsibility settle on his shoulders, but he refused to let it crush him. He had come too far, and now the time to celebrate had come.

As he glanced around the hall, his gaze met Maeve's from across the large chamber. Her green eyes sparkled like emeralds, and her auburn hair framed her face like a fiery halo. In that moment, Ewan was struck by the knowledge that this woman, whom he only just met, held the key to his clan's future.

The key to his own future.

"People of Clan MacDrummond," Ewan began, his voice strong and steady, "I stand before ye today with news that will forever shape our future." He paused for a brief moment, letting the words sink in, his gaze sweeping over their faces, taunt and tense. Fear even lurked here and there, and Ewan realized how worried his people had been since his father's passing. Aye, they had been right to be concerned. As much as their lack of faith in him had pained him, he understood. After all, he, too, had lacked faith in himself, had he not?

Again, Ewan's gaze sought Maeve's, and in the spur of the moment, he said, "Through the help and insight of an extraordinary woman," he inclined his head to her, feeling a swell of gratitude, "and through determined negotiations, we have reached a fair and encouraging agreement with Lord Rutherford."

Murmurs rippled through the hall, surprise etched on the faces of his clans people. Some exchanged incredulous glances while others allowed themselves a tentative smile. Maeve looked suddenly pale, her eyes wide as she seemed to shrink back into the shadows, her gaze fixed on Ewan.

Aye, perhaps he ought to have told her that he wanted to voice his gratitude and admiration openly for her. Yet until this very moment, Ewan had not known himself. He had been too swept away by the events of that day that his mind felt a little slow at present.

Inhaling a deep breath, Ewan smiled at Maeve across the hall, watching his people turn to look upon her, curiosity etched into their faces. Maeve tried her best to smile at them, and yet there was something in her gaze that betrayed her unease. Ewan wondered why that was, for she did not strike him as overly shy or insecure. In fact, if asked, he would swear that she was one of the strongest, bravest people he had ever known.

"Lord Rutherford and I agreed," Ewan went on, seeing the need to further reassure his people, "to assist one another in times of need. After the way Lord Rutherford came to our aid after the war, 'tis now our turn to provide assistance. Because of his kindness, our clan didna go hungry. We survived and were given the chance to thrive once more." He looked at the stern English lord by his side. While there was no obvious delight or relief upon the man's face, Ewan now thought to see subtle emotions hiding just below the surface. "Now, 'tis our turn to show kindness, to share the bounty of our land with those affected by a terrible flood. We shall sent food for as long as it is needed, knowing that first and foremost we are all people on this earth, not Englishmen or Scots. Aye, we shall all be stronger for this alliance."

Lord Rutherford met his eyes and nodded in agreement.

As the full impact of Ewan's words sunk in, that none would be forced across the border to toil English soil, delight bloomed on the faces of his people. Their eyes shone not only with relief but with pride as well, and Ewan felt deeply touched to see them look at him as they had once looked at his father.

The hall erupted into cheers and applause, a cacophony of joy and triumph ringing through the castle. Ewan allowed himself a moment to bask in the warmth of his people's approval while his thoughts, though, remained anchored on the woman who had made all this possible.

Maeve stood near the back of the hall, her expression inscrutable as she watched the celebrations unfold. There was something about her, an aura of mystery and power, that both intrigued and captivated him. Ewan knew he needed her by his side, not just for the sake of the clan, but for his own heart as well.

Forever.

Soon.

Before Ewan could make his way across the hall to her side, though, he spotted Drystan amidst the throng of people, his eyes narrowing as he studied Ewan from the other end of the hall. It seemed as though the man was grappling with an internal struggle—whether to give in to the happiness or cling to his resentment toward Ewan's leadership. Finally, though, Drystan approached him, offering a stiff nod of approval. "Ye've done well, Ewan," he said begrudgingly. "For the clan."

"Thank ye, Drystan," Ewan replied, giving him a nod in return, relieved to have earned the man's respect. Then, though, his gaze once more wandered toward the mysterious woman who had helped turn the tide in his favor.

Maeve still stood in the same spot, her arms folded across her chest as she watched the festivities with a guarded expression. Ewan made his way toward her, pushing through the crowd of jubilant clansmen who offered him pats on the back and congratulatory cheers. When he finally reached her, Ewan took Maeve's hand in his and pulled her into a grateful embrace. "Thank ye, Maeve. I couldna have done this without ye," he whispered, his breath stirring the little hairs upon her temple.

"Ye're welcome, Ewan" Maeve murmured, a slight tremor to her voice and the smile upon her face oddly strained.

"Are ye all right?" Ewan asked, feeling an odd weight settle upon his heart as he looked deeply into her enchanting green eyes, feeling a connection that transcended mere gratitude. Still, there was a part of Maeve that she kept to herself.

"I'm fine," she replied, and the corners of her lips strained upward, forming a wider smile; yet it still seemed as burdened as before. Did she perhaps doubt him? His affection for her?

Ewan exhaled a slow breath. "I love ye, Maeve," he murmured, his voice wavering with vulnerability as he spoke the words he ought to have uttered the moment their paths crossed, "and I want ye by my side for the rest of our days. Will ye—?"

Her eyes widened; yet before he could finish the questions, before she could answer, a group of boisterous clansmen surrounded them both, clapping Ewan on the back and insisting he join in yet another toast to their successful negotiation. Reluctantly, Ewan allowed himself to be pulled away, certain they would not leave him be until he shared a drink with them. And so, he once more left Maeve standing alone, vowing that tomorrow would see them joined for good.

The celebration lasted long into the night, a joyful cacophony filling the great hall, as members of Clan MacDrummond toasted to their newfound security. Laughter and conversation mixed with the clink of ale-filled tankards, creating a symphony of merriment that echoed off the ancient stone walls. Ewan could feel the energy in the room while his heart swelled with pride and relief.

When he found his bed, still fully-clothed, Ewan did not know; however, sometime in the early hours of dawn, he awoke with a start, his heart pounding in his chest. The dying embers of the fire cast eerie shadows on the walls of his bedchamber, and the wind howled mournfully outside. He shook off the last tendrils of sleep as a sense of urgency gripped him.

Maeve's face swam before his eyes, her green gaze filled with sadness, and he felt an inexplicable certainty that something was terribly wrong. *Farewell, Ewan*, her voice seemed to whisper in his mind, carried on the ghostly wind.

Panic coursed through him, and without wasting another second, Ewan threw off the covers and rushed out into the dark, drafty corridor.

His feet barely touched the cold stone floor as he sprinted toward Maeve's chamber, fear and determination propelling him forward. As he reached her door, his breath came in ragged gasps, and his heart hammered against his ribs. Desperation clawed at his insides as he flung it open, only to find the room empty and silent.

"Maeve!" he called out, though he knew deep down that she was gone, and a cold sense of loss settled over him, chilling him to the bone. His gaze darted around the chamber, searching for any trace of her, but there was nothing—it was as if she had vanished into thin air. Was that not how he had found her? Had she not suddenly been in his path as though risen from the ground?

Yet she *was* a woman of flesh and blood, and she could not possibly have vanished into thin air. Nay, she had left of her own volition, slipped out into the night because...

Ewan closed his eyes. "What is yer secret, Maeve?" he murmured to the empty chamber, his voice strained with worry as he tried to quell the rising panic within him. "What terrifies ye so that ye rather leave than confide in me?" He could not lose her now, not when he had only just found her. But what could he do? Where could she have gone?

"Think, Ewan, think!" he berated himself, running a hand through his disheveled hair. "Ye must find her. Ye canna let her leave like this." As he struggled to comprehend what had happened, a torrent of emotions engulfed him—fear, confusion, and above all, an overwhelming sense of loss.

A heavy weight settled in Ewan's chest as he gazed at Maeve's empty room. The cold wind whispered through the window, echoing the farewell that still haunted his thoughts, and he stood there for a moment, feeling more alone than he ever had before.

Farewell, Ewan, her voice rang in his head again. *I wish I could stay, but I dunna belong here*.

With a sudden surge of intuition, Ewan knew where Maeve had

gone. After all, at least as far as he knew, she had no other place in this world. And whether or not she wished to leave, Ewan knew he could not simply give up. He could not lose her without a fight.

He paused for only an instant then rushed out the door, his resolve hardening like steel within him. If Maeve had left the castle, he would find her—no matter what it took. For at that moment, Ewan MacDrummond realized that he would willingly face any danger, any challenge, just to keep her by his side.

She was his...

... as he was hers.

Chapter Seventeen

TWO AS ONE

Moonlight streamed through the castle window, casting a pale glow on Maeve's tear-streaked face as she slipped out of her chamber. Her heart pounded in her chest, each heartbeat echoing the weight of her decision to leave. She could not bear the thought of Ewan rejecting her if he ever discovered the truth about her ability; it was better to preserve her cherished memories of him untainted by his disdain. Clutching her meager belongings to her chest, Maeve stole down the darkened halls, fear clawing at her once more. "Please forgive me, Ewan," she whispered, her voice barely audible even to herself.

When she reached the edge of the forest, Maeve hesitated, glancing back one last time at the imposing fortress that had become her refuge. A sob caught in her throat as she turned away and disappeared into the shadows of the trees, feeling like a ghost returning to its grave.

Aye, returning to the forest felt familiar, each step awakening memories of the life she had had only days prior. Yet Maeve felt no sense of relief at returning home. In fact, she felt as though she were bidding her home farewell for good. Not even when her eyes fell upon her little shelter, tucked away in the hidden clearing, did her heart stir with anything but regret. "Am I making a big mistake?" Maeve murmured to the raven perched atop one of the branches nearby, its obsidian eyes watching her most carefully. "Am I wrong to go without a word?"

Maeve hung her head, torn between fear and hope, between the disappointments of her past and the tentative faith that had slowly grown within her heart since crossing Ewan's path.

"Is this truly the only way?" Maeve wondered aloud, her voice trembling. She longed to return to Ewan's side, to feel his strong arms wrapped around her and hear his gentle laughter warming her soul. "Is there any chance he would forgive me for my secrets? Any at all?" Aye, in her dreams, Maeve had seen such a moment, and yet in the harsh light of day, her soul could not imagine the moment, could not imagine ever standing strong enough to share them. No doubt, her dreams would falter and fade and turn dark.

The wind rustled through the leaves above her, whispering their melancholy melody. The song of the woods had once been her only companion, yet now it seemed to mock her solitude. Her heart ached as her fingers brushed against the soft fabric of the dress Ewan had gifted her, the sensation of his touch lingering in the threads.

"Stop it, Maeve," she admonished herself, her green eyes glistening with unshed tears. "He isna yers to keep. Ye must let him go."

But even as she tried to convince herself that leaving was the best course of action, doubt gnawed at her heart. There was still a part of her that craved his love and acceptance, a yearning that would not be silenced even by the most logical of arguments.

"Mayhap..." she whispered into the dawn hours of the day, her voice barely carrying on the wind. "Mayhap there is still hope for us." She closed her eyes. "Or mayhap not."

Maeve's hands trembled as she tried to fold the simple woolen shawl she had worn so many times. The world around her blurred as fresh tears threatened to spill from her eyes. Closing them, she took a deep breath, willing herself to be strong for what lay ahead.

"Running away will do ye nay good, Maeve."

The deep voice behind her made Maeve jolt, and she spun, clutching the shawl to her chest.

Ewan MacDrummond stood before her, his towering figure framed by the trees that surrounded the small clearing. He was every inch the laird he had been born to be, with his broad shoulders, ebony hair, and stormy grey eyes that seemed to see right through her even in the dim light of early morning.

"Wh-what are ye doing here?" she stammered, taking a step back as he approached, her heart jumping with joy and aching with fear all at once.

"Ye dinna think I would let ye go without a fight, did ye?" Ewan's eyes were filled with determination and concern as he reached out to grasp her elbow, halting her retreat. Yet Maeve also glimpsed a touch of pain and... betrayal.

Maeve swallowed hard. "Let me go," she pleaded, struggling against his iron grip. "I have to leave, Ewan. Ye'll never understand—"

"Then help me understand, Maeve!" he implored, desperation etched across his face as he grasped her arms with both hands. "Why are ye running away? What is it ye're so afraid of? What can ye not tell me?"

"Ye shouldna be here," Maeve whispered, her heart hammering in her chest, yearning to run away as far as she could and at the same time throw herself into his arms without even a moment's delay. "How did ye find me?"

Ewan's expression softened, his grip on her arms loosening, and his brows drew down in confusion. "I dunna quite ken," he murmured, searching her face. "I woke to hear yer voice whispering in my mind, bidding me farewell." His grey eyes held hers, seeking answers. "I heard ye as loud and clear as though ye'd stood right beside me." He swallowed. "How is that possible?"

Maeve stared at him, shock rippling through her. She had not willingly sent her thoughts to him; it was something she could not control, at least not yet.

"Ye... heard my thoughts?" she asked, her limbs trembling like leaves.

Yet again Ewan's brows drew down ever so slightly as he looked into her face. "Ye're not surprised," he murmured more to himself than her. Then he blinked and shook his head as though to rid himself of the confusion her murmurs had caused. "Not truly." Again, his grip on her arms tightened and he pulled her closer, the tip of his nose almost touching hers. "Tell me," he murmured quietly, his breath fanning over her lips.

Maeve's heart ached, torn between her fear of rejection and her love for this man who had shown her more kindness than anyone else in her life. She looked into his grey eyes, searching for any sign that he might still care for her despite the way she had slunk away in the night.

Despite the secrets he sensed nearby.

Maeve took a deep breath and looked into Ewan's eyes. "I dunna ken how I sent my thoughts to ye, Ewan," she admitted, her voice soft and hesitant, her heart beating so fast that for a moment she feared she might faint. "I didna even ken I could do it, not until recently when ye told me ye heard my voice whisper to ye."

Ewan remained very still, his gaze fixed upon hers. "Yet there is more," he whispered, his gaze expectant. "Tell me."

Maeve nodded in acquiescence. "I… I can hear the thoughts of those around me." She swallowed hard, seeing the slight widening of his eyes, yet he said nothing but waited for her to continue. "'Tis something that has been with me since I was a wee lass. I dunna ken why, but I can hear the thoughts of others, like whispers in the wind."

Ewan inhaled a slow breath, his gaze never leaving hers. Then he nodded. "It caused ye pain, did it not?" he asked, surprising her with the soft, soothing tone of his voice. "Ye lost yer home and yer family because of it, is that not so? 'Tis why ye are so fearful."

Tears streamed down Maeve's face, and for a moment, she barely managed a nod.

Then Ewan's hands moved from her arms to cup her face, the pads of his thumbs gently brushing over her cheekbones. "Tell me," he said yet again.

"When I was ten, my village discovered my… my ability." Maeve blinked her eyes fiercely, needing to see Ewan's face, needing to see the truth in his eyes. "They were terrified, called me a witch, and blamed me for every misfortune that befell them. One day, they became so enraged that they set fire to our home while my family slept inside." She squeezed her eyes shut as she remembered the night that had forever changed her life. "We escaped the flames, and my parents packed up a few things they managed to save. They wished to start over elsewhere, begin again." She swallowed hard, remembering the hard expression in her mother's eyes. "Without me." Her voice broke, and yet the words tumbled forth. "They took my younger siblings, leaving me behind, and simply walked away. I never saw them again." Her knees gave out then, the pain of abandonment still raw after all these years.

Ewan caught her, though, his grey eyes wide with shock and disbelief, and Maeve feared that this revelation would be the final straw, that he would turn away from her now and abandon her just as everyone else had in her life.

"Ye may go now, Ewan," Maeve murmured as he held her in his arms, her head resting against his shoulder. "I understand if ye can no longer care for me." She struggled to free herself from his hold, her hands pushing against his large chest, when in truth all she wanted was to snuggle closer.

Yet Ewan refused. His arms remained, holding her tightly, his eyes seeking hers. "Ye're a wise woman in many ways," he murmured, a touch of humor to his voice, and Maeve even thought to see the ghost of a smile tease his lips. "Yet ye're a fool if ye think that anything in this world or beyond will ever sway me from yer side."

Thunderstruck, Maeve stared at him, wondering if she had perhaps lost her mind or yet again strayed into a dream.

"Maeve, I am so sorry for the pain ye have suffered," Ewan murmured, his voice heavy with empathy and understanding. "I canna begin to imagine the isolation and fear ye must have felt, but I swear to ye, I will never turn my back on ye."

Despite her disbelief, Maeve could not help but feel a flicker of hope as she looked into the depths of his eyes. "Ye canna mean that."

He chuckled. "Aye, I can. And I do." Gently, he set her back upon her feet, his hands firmly grasping her shoulders should her legs give out again. "I understand that ye're fearful, but ye needa understand that there is nothing, no reason that can make me turn from ye." He pulled her closer and dipped his head to look deep into her eyes. "Do ye hear me? Nothing." He swallowed. "I love ye, Maeve, and I meant what I said last night. I want ye by my side. I *need* ye by my side." He shook his head to emphasize his words. "I willna let ye go. Nothing's changed. Not for me."

As Ewan's words washed over her, Maeve felt the crushing weight of her past begin to lighten. For the first time in her life, she dared to believe that perhaps she was not meant to be alone after all. And with Ewan by her side, they would face whatever challenges lay ahead, hand in hand, hearts united. "But... yer people? Ewan, what if others find out? I couldna bear it if something were to happen to ye because of me."

"Listen to me, Maeve," Ewan said firmly, holding her gaze with an intensity that belied the tenderness in his voice. "I love ye. More than I ever thought possible. Now more than ever, I ken that we canna live in fear. Ye taught me that all people have good in them, that where it matters we're all the same." He straightened, his gaze filled with determination. "Nothing ye say will sway me, Maeve. I ken what I want, and that is ye."

Maeve stared at him, her eyes widening in disbelief. She searched his face, looking for any sign that he might be misleading her, but all she saw was the unwavering sincerity in his stormy grey eyes. Her breath caught in her throat, and she felt her heart quicken.

"Will ye marry me, Maeve?" Ewan asked then, his voice earnest and full of emotion. "Let us build a life together, built on trust and love. Let me stand beside ye, help ye navigate through yer fears and doubts as ye have helped me through mine."

The words hung heavy in the air between them, a proposal so unexpected that Maeve's mind went blank, unable to comprehend what she had just heard. She blinked back tears, her chest tightening as conflicting emotions warred within her.

"But Ewan, yer people... I..."

His hands cupped her face yet again, his skin warm and reassuring against her chilled cheeks. "Ye dunna have to share yer secret with anyone if ye dunna wish to. I will always respect yer wishes, and in time, we will see where life takes us."

Maeve looked into his eyes, seeing the promise of a future filled with understanding, love, and companionship, and her heart longed for it with such power that her knees buckled again. She sank into Ewan's arms without another thought, and he caught her. She felt the warmth of his body as he held her close, his heartbeat a steady rhythm beneath her ear. Her own heart fluttered within her chest, torn between fear and elation. The idea of marrying Ewan, of being accepted by him despite her secret, sent her pulse racing with hope.

"Will ye marry me, Maeve?" Ewan asked again, his voice a soft rumble, imbued with both tenderness and determination. His grey eyes bore into hers, seeking the truth she hid behind a wall of fear.

A single tear escaped from the corner of her eye, betraying her vulnerability. She bit her lip, grappling with the weight of the decision. She knew that by accepting his proposal, she was not only risking her own life and welfare and happiness—but also his own. It was a leap of faith she never thought she could take. Yet if she did not, was that not an equally great risk?

"A-Aye," Maeve stammered finally, her gaze locked with his. "Aye, Ewan. I love ye, and I will marry ye."

The expression on Ewan's face transformed in an instant. His eyes brightened, joy radiating from every pore. He pulled Maeve into his arms, her feet leaving the ground as he spun her around in a circle, their laughter mingling with the rustle of leaves above. "Ye've made me the happiest man alive, mo chridhe," he whispered breathlessly, setting her down but not releasing her from his embrace. "I promise ye, we will build a life together where ye feel safe, loved, and cherished."

Maeve's heart swelled at his words, and for the first time in years, she allowed herself to believe in the possibility of a future free from fear and isolation. For in the end, love proved more powerful than fear—a force that even the Old Ones would struggle to conquer.

Chapter Eighteen

A PLACE CALLED HOME

The sun shone brightly over Castle MacDrummond, casting its golden rays on the ancient stones and surrounding hills. Ewan felt a warmth in his chest as he stood at the makeshift altar, the autumn breeze rustling his black hair. The entire clan had gathered to bear witness to their laird's wedding, and the joyful atmosphere was infectious.

Maeve approached, her auburn hair flowing down her back like a fiery cascade, complemented by the simple yet elegant gown that hugged her curves. Her striking green eyes met his, and Ewan found himself lost in them for a moment before he regained his composure. As they exchanged their vows, the wind seemed to carry their words across the rolling hills, binding them not only to each other but to the very land itself.

"Ye are now my wife," Ewan said softly, sealing their union with a tender kiss. "Ye're mine as I am yers."

Maeve's eyes sparkled with mischief, a side to her Ewan was only now discovering that she was beginning to feel more at ease within Clan MacDrummond. "And ye're mine to kiss whenever I wish," she murmured as their people cheered around them, Maeve's hands warm within his own.

Ewan chuckled as he leaned in and whispered in her ear. "If ye sought to shock me, lass, ye'll be disappointed."

With the ceremony concluded, the celebration commenced within the castle walls. Laughter and music filled the air, and the scent of roasted meats and freshly baked bread wafted through the halls. Ewan's heart swelled with pride as he observed the clan embracing Maeve as one of their own, tentative at first but soon with increasing determination.

Aunt Innes, the ever-critical matriarch, approached them with a rare smile on her wrinkled face. "Ye make a bonnie couple, ye do," she said, clasping Maeve's hands in her own. "Welcome to our family, lass."

"Thank ye, Aunt Innes," Maeve replied, her cheeks flushed with happiness.

Even Drystan, who had been nothing but disdainful toward Ewan's leadership, raised a cup in toast to the newlyweds, and Cromartie clapped him on the shoulder, his hardened expression softening for just a moment. "Ye've chosen well, Ewan," he whispered. "She'll make a fine lady of the castle."

As people danced and laughed around them, Maeve and Ewan found a quiet corner to steal a few moments alone. Grasping his wife's hands, Ewan pulled her close, his grey eyes searching hers. "Ye look almost at ease, Maeve," he said, his heart now lighter than it had been in a long time—if only his father were alive to see them today. "I pray that MacDrummond Castle will soon feel like home."

Maeve sighed, leaning closer. "Ye're my home, Ewan. Ye were from the first moment I laid eyes on ye." She placed a kiss upon his lips that made Ewan want to whisk her away then and there. As he grasped her hand, though, she held him back, and her smile wavered slightly. "Ewan, I've been thinking, and I believe 'twould be wise to keep my... ability a secret—only to be used in times of great need." She glanced at their people, their faces aglow with joy, their spirits carefree and unburdened. "I fear 'twould unsettle the clan to know their thoughts are not entirely their own."

Ewan nodded in agreement. He had come to the same conclusion, and yet he would never have dreamed of taking this decision out of Maeve's hands. Perhaps one day, the time would come for her to feel safe enough to share all that she was with their clan. For now, though, Ewan was happy that she did so with him. "Of course, my love," he replied, his voice gentle. "As ye wish. Yer secret is safe with me, and it will be until ye decide otherwise."

And with that, Ewan tugged his new wife forward, and they ducked out through a side entrance, laughing as they stole away from their own wedding festivities, eager to be in each other's arms, ready to embark on their new life as husband and wife.

Epilogue

Five years later

Maeve stood by the windows of her solar and gazed out at the walled-in castle garden, entranced by the sight of her wee son. Cormag, with his raven-black hair and hawk-like gray eyes, was a mirror image of his father, his quiet thoughtfulness and tender care in everything he did a great joy to both his parents. Aye, Ewan was already certain that Cormag would make a fine laird one day. Maeve, though, did not like looking quite so far ahead.

Almost immobile, Cormag crouched by the edge of the garden wall, his gaze fixed on something Maeve could not see. Then, slowly, as though he were carried by a gentle breeze, he inched forward, his right hand outstretched. His face looked tense, his little brows drawn together as though overshadowed by pain.

Then, he sat back, settling himself on the ground, a small creature gently cradled in his hands. "Look at him, Ewan," Maeve said softly, beckoning her husband to join her at the window. "Is this a squirrel?"

Squinting his eyes, Ewan looked at his son. "Aye, I suppose 'tis. 'Tis injured, though."

Maeve smiled. "And he's tending to it," she murmured, pride warming her heart to see her son so dedicated to a creature's needs. His tender touch and the furrowed brow of concentration upon his little face revealed the depth of his compassion. "He has such a gentle soul."

Ewan exhaled a deep sigh that rang with fondness and the same pride Maeve felt in her own chest. "Aye, that he does." He wrapped his arms around her waist, resting his chin on her shoulder as they both gazed upon their child. "Aye, he takes after his mother in that regard," he whispered, pressing a kiss to her temple.

As they watched their son, Maeve let her thoughts wander to her own ability—the power that had once isolated her from the rest of the world. She wondered if Cormag might have inherited those same gifts.

Or perhaps similar ones.

"Ewan," she hesitated, voicing her concern. "Do ye think our lad might have... abilities, like mine?" She turned to meet her husband's eyes. "Perhaps the Old Ones considered him worthy?" Aye, the old stories still resonated within Maeve's heart, easing her concern for her son's future. Of course, she would not begrudge him his own gift; however, neither could she help the worry that came to her heart at the thought of him equally isolated as she had once been.

Ewan considered her question for a moment before responding. "I dunna ken, Maeve. But even if they did, we'll be there to guide him, to love him, and to help him understand his place in this world." He cupped her cheeks, and the expression in his grey eyes told her that he understood. "We'll face it together, just as we always have. He'll not be alone. Not ever."

Maeve nodded, taking comfort in Ewan's words, and she closed her eyes, letting out a breath, feeling both grateful and apprehensive for the future. "Ye're right, Ewan," she murmured as she turned in her husband's embrace, leaning back against him as her gaze once more sought her son. "Together, we'll be able to face whatever lies ahead."

Together, they watched Cormag rise to his feet, the squirrel gently cradled in his arm. When he looked up and caught them looking, a proud smile touched his face, and he waved to them with his free hand, his innocent joy infectious.

Ewan and Maeve waved back, their hearts swelling with love for their precious child. No matter what might lie ahead, they would face it together.

As a family.

As always.

The End

Maeve and Ewan's epic tale may be over, but Cormag's has only just begun...

Scottish laird Cormag MacDrummond lives only for his clan's welfare, denying his heart's deepest desires. But offering refuge to alluring outcast Moira Brunwood proves his undoing.

Read *Banished & Welcomed – The Laird's Reckless Wife*.

About Bree

BREE WOLF is a USA Today bestselling author and award-winning word wizard, who is rarely seen without a book in hand or fingers glued to the keyboard. Searching for her true calling, Bree valiantly battled the hallowed halls of academia, earning a BA in English, an MA in Specialized Translation, and countless paper cuts. After wandering abroad and toiling at translation agencies and law firms in Ireland, she realized her heart belonged to one place only: the pages of a good romance novel.

With over 50 published works, Bree has crafted a myriad of intricately woven worlds where resilient heroines find once-in-a-lifetime love with complicated heroes. Through tales of heartbreak and triumph, her characters persevere to hard-won happily-ever-afters, taking readers along on the poignant journey.

Whether in Regency England, medieval castles or the drama of Highland lairds, Bree's gift is capturing romance's full emotional spectrum. Her stories sweep across landscapes and centuries but always promise hard-fought hope for heroes and heroines to find that magical blend of laughter, sorrow, passion and partnership that is true love.

A lifelong bookworm and language enthusiast, Bree is devoted to love stories that linger in a reader's heart long after the last page. Her own heart beats through every tale promising romance as the greatest adventure.

If you're an avid reader, sign up for Bree's newsletter on www.breewolf.com as she has the tendency to simply give books away. Find out about freebies, giveaways as well as occasional advance reader copies and read before the book is even on the shelves!

Connect with Bree and stay up-to-date on new releases:

facebook.com/breewolf.novels
x.com/breewolf_author
instagram.com/breewolf_author
amazon.com/Bree-Wolf/e/B00FJX27Z4
bookbub.com/authors/bree-wolf

www.ingramcontent.com/pod-product-compliance
Lightning Source LLC
LaVergne TN
LVHW091326190726
843491LV00002B/592